PURSUIT

Western Stories

PURSUIT

Western Stories

VERNE ATHANAS

Edited by

JON TUSKA

Five Star
Unity, Maine

Other copyright information may be found on page 216.

Five Star Western.
Published in 1999 by arrangement with
Golden West Literary Agency.

Cover photograph by Johnny D. Boggs

December 1999

First Edition

Five Star Standard Print Western Series.

The text of this edition is unabridged.

Set in 11 pt. Plantin by Al Chase.

Printed in the United States on permanent paper.

Library of Congress Cataloging-in-Publication Data
Athanas, Verne.
    Pursuit : western stories / by Verne Athanas ; edited by
Jon Tuska. — 1st ed.
        p.   cm.
    "Five Star western" — T.p. verso.
    Contents: Ointment for Mangas — The day of Saint
Andrew — The pioneers — A woman to be whipped —
Red fury — Killer at large — Pursuit.
    ISBN 0-7862-1842-8 (hc : alk. paper)
    1. Frontier and pioneer life — West (U.S.) Fiction.
2. Western stories.   I. Tuska, Jon.   II. Title.
PS3551.T39P87   1999
 813′.54—dc21   99-41701

TABLE OF CONTENTS

FOREWORD

Jon Tuska

He was born William Verne Athanas on August 13, 1917 in Cleft, Idaho. His father was a construction foreman, and so Verne's growing years were spent constantly on the move, wherever his father's present job happened to be. Schooling was sporadic, although he did attend classes long enough in such places as an Oregon logging location designated simply as Camp 2 to learn how to read and write. He once described himself as "a moving target which absorbed very little of the education aimed at me. My braincase being thus uncluttered by education, I have since been able to accumulate therein a great untidy mass of unrelated junk which affords me much bemused entertainment in stirring it around. I never know what's likely to turn up next." His early employment was as unskilled farm labor, including hog-slopping, wire-stringing, and post-hole digging, then on to section-hand, truck driving, speed monkey, railroad brakeman, service station attendant, and, finally, as a stationery salesman. In 1936 he married Alice Spencer. They made their home in Ashland in southern Oregon, and they would have two sons.

Writing, although he never admitted it in print, was a career he came to from necessity rather than by design. At eleven Verne was stricken by rheumatic fever, and this later led to the chronic heart disease that plagued his adult life. He had often scoffed at writers previously. Yet, when he could no longer engage in physical labor of any kind for reasons of health, he himself turned to writing for a living. His first efforts were technical advice articles for the magazine *Popular Mechanics*. By 1948, his first fiction was being published in *Railroad Magazine*, stories that called on his work experiences in logging camps and on railroads. In 1949 his fiction began appearing in *Adventure* and *Blue Book*. These early stories are usually contemporary in setting. In 1950, when Fiction House, a publisher of pulp magazines, launched *Indian Stories*, a quarterly in which Indians of various tribes were to be the principal characters and the stories were to be narrated from the Indian point-of-view, Verne wrote three stories for this short-lived publication, all of which were run in the second issue: "Red Arrow Ambush" by W. V. Athanas, "Brand of the Red Warrior" by Ike Boone, and "Death to the White Sioux" by Anson Slaughter. "Red Arrow Ambush" is the weakest of the three, well researched in terms of Sioux culture and beliefs but rather too episodic to sustain continuity. Interestingly, however, it concludes with the Fetterman massacre, and, being published in the Fall, 1950 number, it appeared the same year and embodies many of the same sympathies as the Will Henry novel, NO SURVIVORS (1950), about the same historical event. "Brand of the Red Warrior" is a far more unified story, yet one that cannot but have a sad note throughout. The tragic figure is Frazee whose Cheyenne name is Buffalo Man. He cannot continue to scout for the Army because of his sympathy for the Cheyennes, but he cannot live with this doomed tribe, either. He becomes an exile from both worlds. In "Death to the White Sioux," a white youth who was adopted by a Sioux chief after Crow captivity is confronted with other whites in a wagon train bound for Oregon and, by the end, makes his decision to remain with his adopted people. Verne continued over the next several years to write short fiction for other Fiction House magazines, under the pseudonyms Anson Slaughter and Ike Boone as well as his own name. Pseudonyms were a requirement at pulp magazines where editors did not want more than one story under any author's name to appear in the Table of Contents for a particular issue.

For other pulp magazines Verne also developed what proved to be a series of stories about Seven-Foot Saunders (who is actually six-foot-eight) and his sidekick, Shorty Shamrock. These stories were published under the byline Bill Colson, in which pseudonym Verne used his mother's maiden name as his authorial surname and the diminutive of his own prænomen. These light-hearted tales usually centered on the dynamics of the relationship between the principal characters as much as on their various adventures together. Verne also made use of his experiences in logging camps in creating the contemporary logger, Moose McGinty, and the author's technical grasp of logging is readily apparent in stories such as "Up Comes McGinty" in *New Western* (1/52) and "Down Went McGinty" in *.44 Western* (5/52), both pulps published by Popular Publications. But it was first in Western fiction Verne published in slick magazines—such as "The Conestoga Bells" in *Country Gentleman* (6/51) and "The Richest Vein" in *Collier's* (7/28/51)—that he moved beyond the somewhat juvenile purview of so much Western fiction with its clear distinctions between good guys and bad guys, and these later stories have both a decided maturity of theme and feature characters of far greater complexity, as had previously been true of the Western magazine fiction written by another distinguished Oregon author, Ernest Haycox, who died in 1950 and whose once preëminent position was carried on in slick magazines in the 1950s by five principal authors: Frank Bonham, Peter Dawson, T. T. Flynn, Jack Schaefer, and Verne Athanas.

If there is a predominant theme in much of Verne

Athanas's short fiction in the decade of the 1950s, it is the specter of relentless determination required of a person in winning through in a life-struggle with the land and the hostile human environment encountered in the American West. He was also attracted to variations of the initiation story. In "Crimson Crossing" in *Fifteen Western Tales* (9/52), young Jonny Free hires on with a small wagon train because he wants to go West. He proves his mettle in a confrontation at a wooden bridge over what is called Murderer's Creek because he is smarter and tougher than those who have staked it out to extort money from emigrants who need to cross it. The same sort of spirit inflames young Jim Smith in "Maverick in the Bunkhouse" in *Argosy* (9/52) who hires on at the C R ranch. One of the hands picks a fight with Jim only to become terrified once he realizes that the only thing that can stop Jim, once he has been prodded, would be to kill him. Another story from that same year, "Killer's Dark" in *Adventure* (1/52), has a slight alteration of this same theme. The protagonist is a bank robber who unwittingly kills a lawman's son when making his getaway. Jess Lucey, the bank robber, knows that "Abel Bane would follow him until he fell, and, when he was fallen, he would crawl, for that was the mold in which Abel Bane was cast."

"The Pioneers" in *Zane Grey's Western Magazine* (4/53) is one of Verne's most compact and dramatic stories, and it has been included here. It tells of Byron Martin's pursuit of renegade Rogue Indians who left him for dead and stole his wife and young son. This experience, however traumatic, builds character in this man and this woman. In "The Spirit of Katyann," written for inclusion in the Western Writers of America anthology, FRONTIERS WEST (Doubleday, 1959), Verne effectively evoked the supernatural. In this story Katyann is a burro that, after she is killed, returns as a spirit to save her master from certain death at the hands of the man who shot her.

In the course of his relatively brief career, spanning only fourteen years, Verne Athanas published only three novels. In all of them, with greater or lesser success, he sought to expand the conventions of the traditional Western, and in one instance, with ROGUE VALLEY (Simon and Schuster, 1953), he created an exceptional historical narrative. THE PROUD ONES (Simon and Schuster, 1952) came first, and in it Verne managed to introduce themes unusual in the Western story before this time and created some especially vivid characterizations. Cass Silver is marshal of Red Bone and ostensibly the hero. Thad Oglevie, a young wrangler just in town, saves Silver's life during a shoot-out in which he himself is wounded in the leg and henceforth must walk with a limp and will never again be able to straddle a horse. Cass takes Thad under his wing, training him in his profession and eventually making him his deputy. Cass sleeps with Nancy Kane, a madam in a brothel who genuinely loves Silver, but he will not live with her. Thad vies for the attention of Dorothy Markham, a storekeeper's daughter. Cass is pitted against a powerful saloon boss who manages to have him killed. Cass was a man of relentless determination, but so is Thad as he sets about bringing the saloon boss to justice. Dorothy, however, wants a different kind of man than Thad has become, and to win her love he must finally surrender his badge. THE PROUD ONES (20th-Fox, 1956), directed by Robert D. Webb and starring Robert Ryan and Virginia Mayo, was based on this novel.

Verne Athanas was of the opinion that the basic elements and characters of THE PROUD ONES also seemed to have been the inspiration for the first "adult Western" ever to be heard on radio. "Gunsmoke" was initially broadcast on April

26, 1952 in an episode titled "Billy the Kid" and featuring William Conrad as U. S. Marshal Matt Dillon, Parley Baer as the limping deputy, Chester Proudfoot, Georgia Ellis as Kitty Russell, and Howard McNear as Doc Adams. In this conviction I believe Verne was mistaken. In GUNSMOKE: A COMPLETE HISTORY (McFarland, 1990) by SuzAnne Barabas and Gabor Barabas, the origins of "Gunsmoke," admittedly the first and perhaps still the finest Western dramatic series on radio and television alike (and certainly the longest-running), appear already to have been in the early stages of development in 1947 with the first audition program being recorded as early as June 11, 1949. Yet, there is no denying the similarities between the basic characters in THE PROUD ONES and "Gunsmoke." Ironically, the motion-picture version of THE PROUD ONES, appearing as it did fully four years after the première of "Gunsmoke" on radio and one year after its advent on television, did make it seem to some that the film perhaps owed more to the creators of "Gunsmoke" than to Verne Athanas's novel.

Verne dedicated ROGUE VALLEY to Alice "for all the wonderful years we have had" and even included Alice's grandfather, Aden Spencer, as a character for a bit of dialogue. The novel is set in the Jacksonville district of Oregon after the Civil War. The protagonist is Jed Teppard who, with his brother Toby, returns after fighting for the Confederacy. Oregon is accurately depicted as then it was with its taxes on Mexicans and Chinese so they would not offer significant labor competition to whites, the prevalent distrust of the Rogue Indians (even though the war with them and their removal was by this time in the past), and the rampant (if seemingly contradictory) prejudice against Southern sympathizers. The characterizations are particularly well-etched, and the nemesis for Jed and Toby is a man who is psychologically disturbed, a happenstance occurring also in novels written at the time by Les Savage, Jr., T. T. Flynn, and Alan LeMay. The setting in ROGUE VALLEY is especially rich with its scenes of mining claims and a small-pox epidemic that lays siege to Jacksonville. Bonnie Claire, with whom Jed falls in love, is probably Verne Athanas's most memorable female character.

MAVERICK (Dell, 1956) was Verne Athanas's last novel. It was the expansion of a four-part magazine serial titled "Trail East" that had appeared in *Country Gentleman* beginning with the September, 1951 issue. It is a cattle drive story that does not particularly benefit from the added padding, since this tends to compromise much of the vital tension by adding unnecessary scenes and extended descriptions. On the surface MAVERICK would seem to be a ranch romance in which Clay Lanahan is the ramrod of a trail herd who falls in love with Eileen Prather. Yet the male character more interesting than either Clay Lanahan or Homer Flagg (who is in competition with Clay and engaged to Eileen Prather at the beginning) is the man known only as Tennessee, a truly daring and capable frontiersman who saves Clay's life once on the trail and, even though it means his own death, again at the end.

Authors of Western stories in this period always had to keep themselves aware of the guidelines imposed by magazine and book editors on what was allowable in a Western story and what was considered too off-trail. In order to make a living writing Western fiction, Verne Athanas did devise stories that appeared to follow these editorial guidelines, but he also did something that was rather unusual. He tended, especially in his longer stories, to include a covert story that, while present, may not have seemed pressingly evident to a casual reader. THE PROUD ONES is really very much the covert story of Cass Silver and Nancy Kane, the brothel madam, and MAVERICK is really the covert story of Tennessee. Surely it was by means of these characters in his best Western fiction that Verne Athanas succeeded in altering the customary polarities that had become so standardized. Cass, Nancy, and Tennessee are what I would call "in between" characters, presaging the greater realism and awareness of multiple perspectives that have characterized the best Western stories published more recently.

Why didn't Verne write more novels? Perhaps one reason might have been that short stories do not require such a long commitment of time, an important consideration when life itself has come to seem so temporary and so fragile. He was actively involved with the Western Writers of America and held the post of membership chairman. On June 21, 1962 he was the master of ceremonies at the annual meeting of this organization in Boise, Idaho. After introducing the new president and returning to his table, Verne turned ashen gray. T. V. Olsen was one of the Western writers who was sitting at the same table. He became aware of Verne's condition, and Alice turned to Verne just as he slumped over with a fatal heart attack. Notwithstanding that Ted Olsen had written often of sudden death, never before had he been an eyewitness to it. Years later, Ted confided to me that it was this event that had introduced a new sensitivity in his fiction toward that specter who has no altar and no hymn of praise and from whom all entreaty is deflected.

ROGUE VALLEY remains a novel that belongs in any basic library of the best Western novels from the 1950s, while the best short Western fiction of Verne Athanas definitely deserves to be collected. PURSUIT is the first such collection. With the exception of "Killer at Large," one of several short stories Verne Athanas wrote that has not been previously published in any form, the stories that have been selected for inclusion here appeared first in various magazines where, many times, editors had to adjust the texts to contour a story to the profile of a magazine's readership or to the physical format of the periodical to accommodate unexpected blocks of advertising. The versions of the stories appearing in PURSUIT have been restored, according to the author's original typescripts. In his concern for the complexities, passions, and terrors of the human soul on the American frontier and in his care for accuracy of historical detail, Verne Athanas was an author very much preoccupied with truly timeless themes and the perplexities, always, of the human condition. Having read a good deal of Verne's private correspondence and his personal diaries, as well as so many of his stories, I am able to say of him that he believed a sense of humor is the unique saving grace in a hard, competitive world, that a little laughter makes bearable life at its worst, and that even the seemingly basest of human beings does possess the latent possibility for nobility of thought and action. As one who has lived longer in Oregon than anywhere else in my life, I can appreciate Clay Lanahan's question in MAVERICK: " 'They got a saying . . . that the man who tries to prophesy Oregon weather is either a fool or a newcomer. How long you been here, George?' " In the end, Verne Athanas's penchant for humor and his belief in the possibility of nobility in human character were things he kept foremost as he fashioned his stories and by such means as these gave them, truly, a life of their own.

OINTMENT FOR MANGAS

He had been expecting it, but still it happened awfully fast. One moment he was scuffing along at his easy trot, and the next the Apache buck was hanging in mid-air over him, and coming down from a vaulting leap over the rock. It was close—too close. Lucey got the pistol up in time to slide the slicing hatchet blade aside, but this kind of dog-fighting was what the Apache did best. Off balance, the Apache was letting his body go on past, limply, ready to take his tumbler's fall and come up from the side.

No good. No good at all. Lucey dragged up and back, with the thick pistol butt deep in his fist, and the high front sight caught on the buck's neck and dragged and checked him for just a tiny fraction of a second. Then he brought his heavy knife around in a wiping motion, not putting much thrust on the blade, letting the razor edge do its own work.

The buck felt it too late. His muddy eyes widened, and his mouth opened in a soundless squall. He arched his back convulsively, whipping himself into an arc without leverage to throw himself back, and then his belly muscles gave way, and his guts spilled out and his spine went with a dry-branch crack. He came down in a huddle that wasn't a man any more, but like a clubbed snake—there was life in him yet, and the hatchet lashed out again. Lucey's black wool pants suddenly fell open from calf to cuff, and a streak of hurt bit at his shin.

He stamped with the other foot, grinding the moccasin sole down hard on the greasy wrist, and he stooped and wiped with the knife again. The buck made a bubbling sound and

16

jerked, and Lucey lifted his foot from the wrist only as he pivoted away. He did not even look back at the Apache.

He didn't stop to investigate the leg, either. It worked, and that was all that counted now. They were out there, more of them—had to be—coursing like hounds, fanned to keep him headed. He kept at his scuffing, limping trot, not showing himself above the jumbled rocks.

It was so damned deadly quiet. He could still hear the faint ringing in his ears from the shot he'd fired away back there. He was a little winded from his run and the short and violent tussle with the buck.

I'm getting too old for this, he thought. And then: *Four loads left in the cylinder. If they don't jump me now, I can make it.*

On the heels of the thought the outraged squall came up from behind. They'd found the buck he'd gutted. He had a sudden chilling thought that there wouldn't be time enough now, but he held himself to his gait. The leg was a steady jumping ache, and the hot, dry air was cutting into the pink moisture of his lungs with every dragging breath.

Through the dog-leg in between the three hulking boulders, then the last open stretch of gravelly sand and scrubby brush. Then the flat whip-crack of the carbine lashed spitefully at him, and the ricochet made its deafening scream almost in his ear.

He went full length onto the ground and yelped: "Hold your fire, you damn' fool. Me . . . Lucey."

He kept scrabbling, working his knees and elbows to slide himself. Hell of a note. Damned bucks hacking at his tail and a trigger-happy recruit up ahead with a carbine.

Time enough. The words should have gotten through even the numb layers of a dumb recruit's brain by now. If they hadn't, it would still be better to take a bullet than what the bucks would give him. He came to his knees and then on up to a crouch, never really having stopped, and heard the recruit's scared, apologetic voice and the *slack-clap* of the carbine's action working.

Even now the muzzle was automatically tracking him in, and he wasn't really sure the rookie had him pegged right until he was across the flat and into the rocks.

"Hell," the recruit said with peevish fear, "you popped out there so fast, and. . . ."

"Yeah," grunted Lucey. "You can do what you damn' please now. There's some of 'em out there behind me. Where's Moynihan?"

The soldier had whipped the carbine muzzle back onto the opening at his first words, knuckles dead-white where they squeezed the skimpy forearm of the weapon, and he said jerkily without looking around: "Down by the horses, I guess. Dammit, I hope he sends another man up here."

"Yeah," said Lucey again, and he limped on down into the bowl through the piled rocks.

Moynihan came to meet him, a tough-faced Irishman so lean and mean and burned and dried out by his years in service that no one would ever peg him for anything but Army, even if they saw him naked in a shower stall. "That shot for you?" he said now in half question and half statement.

Lucey said wryly: "That recruit is pretty lonesome up there."

"He's got the softest spot," returned Moynihan. "I've seen rifle ranges tougher than that." He paused then, as if he hated to make the words. "You've seen the captain?"

"Yeah. He's dead."

Moynihan cursed softly, and his eyes clung to Lucey with a sort of grim desperation. "Bad?"

"They'd messed him up some. I shot him before they got the fire going too hot. They're fast, Moynihan. One of 'em caught up with me on the way back, and I wasn't doin' any lingerin'."

"It was naught but God's mercy," the Irishman said earnestly. "He'd've done the same for you if he could."

"Yeah," said Lucey. Then he raised his head and pointed with his chin down toward the hollow of the basin. "What's the word?"

"Four hit. Two of 'em'll die by tonight. The lieutenant and them damn' civilians are still hashin' it over as to how it all started."

Lucey smiled, a bleak wintry smile that was completely humorless. "They can ask Mangas when he comes after them," he said. "He's out there."

Moynihan said quietly: "And I had enough money to buy out, after that last poker game."

"Yeah. And I hope I live to see that day, Moynihan. I'll be old enough to have seen it all . . . the day you buy out."

"Come on," said the Irishman. "The lieutenant will be wantin' a report."

Lieutenant Marker didn't like Bun Lucey, and that was all right. Lucey didn't like Marker. Which is just the way things go, sometimes. You like a man or you don't, but Marker tried too hard. He was a gentleman, and he'd learned the stuff to give the troops. Treat 'em kindly but firmly, and never forget you're a gentleman. Never abuse a man before his outfit, and you can lead a man where you can't drive him. If you set a good example, the men will follow your lead, and, if a good officer takes care of his men, they'll take care of him. But Marker tried too hard.

He was as dirty and sweaty and unshaven as the rest, now, almost self-consciously so, but he was still trying. The splayed finger marks of his gloves showed where he had beaten at his shirt, and his kerchief was knotted a little care-lessly when he'd put it back after mopping his face.

Wants 'em all to know it's pretty tough, thought Lucey.

Marker turned as they came up, Lucey and Moynihan, and his eyes settled with a sort of intent fascination on Lucey's. But he said first: "You checked that shot, Ser-geant?"

"Darrel mistook Lucey for an Apache, sir."

Marker came back to Lucey and said: "He looks enough like one."—and then smiled to take the sting out of the words. Then seriously: "What word of Captain Lynch?"

Lucey said laconically: "He's dead. I shot him."

A sudden pallor rose under the windburn of Marker's face. "My God, man! If you could get that close, we might have had a chance. . . ."

Lucey let the brutal words come out in a flat, unemotional voice. "They had him half skinned, Lieutenant. His eyes was gone and his hair was afire . . . then I shot him. He was too damn' good a man to go the way they was doin' it. I'd do as much for a dog."

He laid it in with that flat voice, and watched the lieu-tenant. Marker went sick-white around the mouth and said again: "My God."

Lucey waited a moment longer, and then added: "They wasn't none of the rest of 'em around. This is all that's left of the troop, Lieutenant." He waited a moment longer, and, when Marker still did not speak, he asked gently: "What's the next move, Lieutenant?"

That snapped Marker out of it a little, and Lucey could almost see him mentally thumbing through the book. *The wounded. Can't leave them. Short of mounts, anyway. Good de-fensive position, maybe a little too much perimeter. But cavalry is not an efficient defensive weapon. . . .* He turned to Lucey now and said: "Think they'll hit us again? Today, I mean?"

"Pretty sure," said Lucey. "I broke up their party, and they'll be projectin' around to keep busy. Yeah, I reckon they'll hit us."

For the first time, he let himself look past the lieutenant to where the two civilians were hunkered in the meager shade of a slab of boulder. Two miners, Stockstill and the other, holding their aloofness from the troopers, and the troopers ignoring them in their own way. *You bastards,* he thought. *A lot of good men are going to die on your account. Mangas wouldn't give any more than his right arm to get you spitted over a fire.*

Lieutenant Marker said quite suddenly: "We'll try for the flats. Sergeant, pass the word. Double up the wounded with the lightest troopers. Send a corporal to bring in the perimeter, but each man's to keep an eye on his sector until the command to mount."

For a moment Moynihan looked as if he were about to say something, and then he thought better of it. He went away at a trot.

Lucey said mildly: "They're thicker'n fleas down that way, Lieutenant."

"And we're sitting ducks here, Lucey. Will you be ready to move with the troop?"

There was ice in that last, and Lucey felt a hot, little burn of resentment. Out of the book. Lead 'em, don't drive 'em. But chop it off short under 'em if they forget their place. "I'm ready now," Lucey said shortly.

It was something under a mile out of the cañon. The troop made less than half of that. Only it wasn't a troop. It had been half a troop to begin with, what with a disinterested Department and the Sioux raising hell up north, and ten of them, not counting the wounded, had gone when Captain Lynch got his. This time perhaps eighteen of them rallied on the sergeant. Moynihan, lean and mean and tough, his horse shot out from under him, came into the rocks with his pistol and the lieutenant's shirt collar all in one hand, and the other hand running a steady stream of red.

He let the lieutenant drop and squalled in a voice as gritty as a shovel edge on stone: "B Troop! In here. Dismount. Give 'em hell, boys!" He wheeled with the pistol at the end of a stiff arm and knocked a scrambling buck off a boulder with one shot. Another one came right into the troop, whining like a hound, a captured carbine cradled at the hip. Lucey shot him through the belly at less than ten feet, and a trooper made a hurt yell and smashed the buck's head with his carbine butt as the buck's weapon went off almost at his back.

The carbines broke it up, finally, and Moynihan essayed a sidling, stooping run to his dead horse and back. He gnawed at the cork of the flat, little half pint and spat it out. "Twenty mortal days I packed this in my saddlebags," he said. "And wid true strength of character, I touched niver a drop. But I knew 'twould be handy, one day." He ignored his flapping, bloody hand, and tipped up the bottle with the other. His thickened brogue was the only sign he made of his hurt.

He sat down, clamped the flask between his knees, and dug out his spring knife. He lifted his left hand, and the third finger dangled. He flipped the hand to straighten it, and laid it up against the gnarled stem of a handy greasewood. The knife blade slid between meat and hide, his teeth went through his lip, and the finger fell off. He sloshed whiskey on the welling stump, pulled the flap of skin he'd cut over the end, and bound it there with a strip torn with his teeth from his neckerchief.

He took another long swig from the bottle, and looked critically at Lieutenant Marker. He lay where Moynihan had dropped him. An arrow had peeled a flap as wide and long as a man's finger just above the ear on the right side, and a bit of the feathering was plastered with blood to the wound. Moynihan looked at him unemotionally, and then up at Lucey. "Some people have all the luck," he said. He sloshed whiskey at the lieutenant's wound, and Marker unconsciously rolled his head from this fresh bite. With the casual roughness of drenching a horse, Moynihan jammed a thumb into the lieutenant's jaw hinge, pushed the neck of the flask between the parted teeth, and let the last dribble run down the man's throat. Marker came up gagging.

Moynihan said in a flat, carrying voice: "Corporal, tell 'em to fire only at plain targets. They're not seeing that many."

The corporal said—"Yo."—and ran, crouching, toward the noisiest cluster of rock.

Marker sat up, then put his aching head in his hands. A man started screaming now. Lucey wheeled and trotted, threading through the piled rock until he came to three of them, bellied down, old-timers with cartridges ready between the fingers of the left hand, carbines cocked but not firing.

The sound was coming from just past the next screen of rock, the naked screaming of a man in mortal fear and hurt. The middle trooper of the trio looked around as Lucey came up, twisted to dig out a thumb-sized remnant of plug tobacco. He bit it carefully in two, put the rest back in his pocket.

Lucey said: "Who'd they catch?"

"Browder, I think." The trooper's jaw came down hard on the chew, and for just a moment the beard-blurred line of his jaw quivered. Then it took up a steady, rolling motion. "Marked him down about over there, when they first jumped us. Thought he was dead. Went down like a sack of spuds. Too bad he wasn't."

"Yeah," said Lucey.

The trooper chewed and spat and said obliquely: "Any chance?"

Lucey put out a hand for the man's carbine, got it, wriggled over to the slot where two boulders came together, and pushed with the butt on the gravelly hot earth, pushing a little ridge ahead of it, such as a man's elbow might make if he were resting on it to peek out. He flipped the butt in a little flirting motion, and the bullet came screaming through in the same instant. He crawled back.

"They're usin' him for bait," he said briefly, and gave back the man's carbine. The trooper didn't thank him, or even look at him.

A hand gun went *wham . . . wham . . . wham* off to his right, and Lucey looked to see one of the miners, the big one, Red Stockstill, phlegmatically emptying his pistol at something out of sight. He was so casual about it that Lucey didn't catch on until the hammer snapped twice on the empty cylinder.

Stockstill felt Lucey's hand on his shoulder, and he came around with a strangled sound and whipped at Lucey's head with the barrel of the pistol. He was frozen stiff, and didn't really see Lucey at all. Lucey got a hand on the wrist, threw his weight on it, and cracked the whip with the man's heavy bulk. Stockstill took a couple of staggering strides and smacked the flat of his broad back against a boulder. It jarred some sense into him, and he stared at Lucey for a long moment as the blankness went out of his eyes. Then he began to shake.

Lucey said bitterly: "You stinkin' yellow slob!"

Stockstill's lips worked under the dirt and whiskers, and he said: "It was Mangas. I seen him. He looked right at me. I seen him, I tell you!"

"I hope he did," said Lucey. "I hope he got a good look. I

hope he remembered who skinned his back with a bullwhip. I hope, when he gets you, you'll see the rest of 'em . . . that Fraley girl and the two kids and their folks, and Captain Lynch . . . with their bellies open and their eyes gone . . . 'cause, damn you Stockstill, you're the one that done it. You give him his name and half of his meanness . . . and I hope to God you pay for it."

Suddenly Lucey couldn't stomach the sight of the man any longer, and he wheeled violently away and ran crouching to where he'd left Moynihan. The screaming of the man the Apaches had out there in the rocks went on and on.

Lieutenant Marker was on his feet, pale and shaky, but under his own power. He asked a little fuzzily: "They all right over there?"

"They'll hold," said Lucey shortly, "till Mangas gets tired of playin' and comes in after us."

Marker said almost absently—"All right."—but Moynihan looked at Lucey sharply, the hurt of his mangled hand beginning to show around his eyes and mouth. He came closer and inquired softly: "That bad?"

"He's got help coming," Lucey said morosely. "Saw the dust from the other side. What we got left?"

"Twelve up, four down, countin' you, me, and the lieutenant. Ten up, if them damn' civilians don't do more than they have." He took a deep, shaky breath that belied the flat unemotion of his voice. "Six mounts."

Lucey thought bleakly: *We ain't going to make it this time.* The thought took the heat out of the brassy, clubbing sun, put a hint of darkness over the blistering rock and baked earth that made this god-forsaken land. *This time we won't make it.* He checked the dust again. It would be there by night. He saw Red Stockstill again, couldn't avoid seeing him, and the bitter thought coursed through him. *You big, worthless worm-*

souled bastard . . . I hope he gets you. He wouldn't, though. Red would save a bullet to insure that Mangas never got his hands on him.

There was always one like Red around. And one like Mangas. A great brute of an Apache, Mangas, six feet and four inches, a great barrel of a giant's body perched on thick, short, bandy legs and with an ugly gargoyle face. Wild as any animal or any Apache, but basically an easy-going sort who wound up quietly enough on the Agency, and stayed quiet as long as he could go hunting once in a while and go on his *tiswin* drunk once a year.

Red Stockstill and his partner Oscar Braikle were miners, by opportunity, not trade. They didn't find the lode, or even a good strike, and unrewarding labor palled soon enough. They'd raveled out their slight rope of patience when Mangas—who wasn't Mangas then, but an unpronounceable series of chuckling grunts—came slouching into their camp to beg tobacco. They said afterward he was stealing grub. Anyway, they wrestled him down and tied him to a tree bole, and they flayed him with a bullwhip until they were both tired of it. He was still hanging in his bonds on the tree, when they packed up and pulled out.

Nobody ever saw the scars on Mangas's back. He wore a red shirt—always a red shirt and no other color. And he wasn't a reservation buck any more. Some said his beating addled his head, but, if it did, it was single-track addled. He lived to kill white men. Or white women, or white children— or, for that matter, anything that wasn't Apache. Mexican freighters, tending their strings with one eye for their mules and one cocked for Mangas Coloradas, crossed themselves absently and said the fat he fried out of his victims was ointment for his flayed back. If it was, his wounds were never soothed to healing.

26

★ ★ ★ ★ ★

The idea began to come to Lucey as the long day slowly wore out its time. It was cat-and-mouse, now—the Apaches never letting up, but never quite making a rush of it, a constant probing at the perimeter, and the carbines lashing at shadow targets, while the troopers took the pounding of the late, hot sun on their backs. They all knew for sure it was Mangas, now. Half a dozen had seen him.

The flats. Half a mile, more or less. But the gantlet of the cañon put it as far away as the moon. Apaches were infantry. Out in the open, cavalry could, with superior mobility and fire-power, maneuver almost at will. Nobody knew that better than Mangas. That was why he'd made a beacon of the burning Fraley ranch, why he'd let the patrol, and finally the troop, through the cañon. Mangas had even split his force, sent the horses on, at least, to make the dust leading out and away from Fraley's. Good bait. He'd caught Captain Lynch, who was an old hand.

Lucey grunted and went back, the idea still vaguely forming. *It'll have to go just so,* he thought. *There's only six horses.*

He reported the dust to the lieutenant, waited for him to thumb mentally through the book for the answer. There was only one answer to it, come daylight, and Mangas with help. It was dusky enough that the flashes showed every shot. If they didn't try now, they'd wait for morning, since Mangas or any other Apache knew that a man killed at night wandered through eternal darkness. Lucey gave the lieutenant his opinion, and saw Red Stockstill close enough, by the cluster of boulders where two troopers held the horses. The lieutenant chewed his lip, while he thought, and Lucey said a little too loudly and roughly: "You can make up your mind, or wait for him to come butcher you in the morning."

27

Marker put his shocked, stiff stare on him and said sharply: "That's enough. You've made your report."

Lucey snorted in supreme contempt and scuffed over to the horses. He hunkered down in abused silence, and jabbed at the flinty earth with a stick. He raised his head once at a scattering of reports, and looked up at Stockstill.

"Army," Lucey said bitterly. "They send a wet-eared pup out here with brass on his blouse, and he knows it all. Read it in a book. He's goin' to get us all hung over a fire."

"Not me," said Stockstill. He was jittery, but he'd come unfrozen. "Not me," he repeated.

Then Moynihan came over and looked down at them coldly. "We'll move out at midnight," he said. He added flatly: "The lieutenant is takin' your horse for the wounded. Rest of us will foot it."

Lucey said nothing, and Moynihan kept that look on him that was half outrage and half wonder, and finally gave up and went away.

Lucey jabbed with the stick, again, and then said without looking at Stockstill: "They'll make noise enough to cover. They'll pull the devils off this end."

There was a sudden break in Stockstill's breathing.

Lucey said with a surly half defiance: "It's my horse, not the Army's. Reckon I'd just as soon it was me ridin' him as an Army fool."

He could almost feel Stockstill turning it over cautiously in his mind.

"Never make it," Stockstill said finally. "He'd never pull 'em all in."

"One man . . . or two . . . could," Lucey insisted. "By easin' out where they ain't expectin'. I ain't no yellow-leg clodhopper to fall over my own feet. An' give me twenty minutes in the clear, and there ain't no 'Pache buck in the territory goin' to fade me."

"You're crazy," said Stockstill without conviction.

"Mebbe," said Lucey. "But I'm goin' to be right over there in that clump of rock at midnight. You do what you damn' please."

The moon was a day past full, and its brilliance was a curse. Its white glare made shadows all the blacker, and nothing moved without its telltale ink-blot shade writhing long and short, attention-compelling as a flag. By midnight, though, the moon had wheeled across into westering, and the cañon was a fathomless pit athwart the land.

There was one bad part. The horse-holding trooper had got the word, and adamantly refused Lucey his horse. Lucey gave it up and drifted across the pocket and into the rocks, black as the pit now.

Mangas was taking no chances. The night was alive out there with the twittering and chirping of their signals. Some of them even had fires, but back, out of range, and someone was *tunking* a drum far downwind.

He heard Stockstill coming, and, when the man was close, he whispered irritably: "Pick up your feet, man."

Stockstill grunted, and then his querulous whisper came back. "We can't do it without horses."

Lucey put his shrug in his voice. Even at arm's length, Stockstill was only a faint movement in the blackness. "Suit yourself. I'm moving out now." He turned softly and caught Stockstill's following movement within moments.

He caught the billy goat smell of the buck before he could hear or see him, and he went to his knees and brought the knife around at the full sweep of his arm. The buck squalled as the edge bit, and Lucey sliced again and came to his feet and let his moccasins slap without heed to noise.

"Run, dammit," he hissed, and took three long, sliding steps. He went flat at the base of a hulking rock, dragged himself under the bellied overhang. He heard the *slurt-shup* of Stockstill's running feet and, more suddenly than he'd really expected, a gasping agonized grunt from the man—then the soft whispering prowl of moccasins. He caught the smell again: smoke and rank meat and body grease and buckskin soaked with sweat. He came to his knees in one smooth motion and lunged with the blade straight ahead. The buck took it just under the ribs, close to the spine, with no more than a gusty grunt, and came down like a sack of potatoes.

Time enough, Lucey thought, and dragged the pistol out of the dog-leg pouch across his belly. He fired one shot into the body before him and another at random down the way Stockstill had gone, took two running strides, and fired again. Then he got the hell out of there.

Moynihan sent the order down the line: "No talking. No firing . . . not even if he's right at the end of your arm. Keep your interval . . . and god damn it, pick up your feet!" He went from man to man, dim shapes in the dark, whispering it in a vicious snarl. The wounded were mounted and lashed there. The rest of them walked.

Moynihan went back to the head of the file. "Ready," he said.

Lieutenant Marker whispered back: "Lucey?"

Moynihan's blistering whisper carried every horrific syllable he'd learned in twenty years' service. Then up the cañon a hand gun blasted twice, then once again.

There was a ringing silence on the heels of that, and then movement, up on the rim. Twice Moynihan saw shadows, held his fire with iron discipline. The shadows were heading toward the shots. Then a voice came out of the dark almost at his elbow, and Lucey said mildly: "Shall I take the point, Moynihan?"

It was a moment before the Irishman could speak, and then he said: "Just past the lieutenant, Lucey."

They couldn't do it without a little noise, even with the animal's hoofs wrapped in torn tunics. But they made it. Twice they were shot at, and half a dozen times arrows came blindly into the darkness with their vicious, ripping *swish*. But the big noise was behind them.

A man was screaming back there, and the animal yapping of the Apaches came above that. Lieutenant Marker ran at a shambling trot to catch Lucey, and dragged at his arm with a clawing hand.

"God's name, man," he cried in a strangled whisper, "who's that?"

"Stockstill," Lucey said quietly. "Let go my arm, Lieutenant."

"You mean you left him . . . back there?" Marker cried in unbelief.

"They had him, when I left," the scout returned imperturbably. Then his voice had the harsh whip of driven sand in it. "How would you have done it, Lieutenant? Think we'd be walkin' out of here without something kept 'em busy back yonder? And if it makes you sick at your belly, think of them Fraley kids and their mother . . . or Captain Lynch."

"But . . . good Lord!"

"How would you have done it, Lieutenant?" Lucey demanded again. He shrugged Marker's hand off his arm, and melted away in the dark. The file whispered its motion behind him, walking in the deathly saving shadow. In the flats, they'd make it. Six old hands mounted could escort the rest of them to the very gates of hell—and make Mangas Coloradas like it.

The lieutenant would get over it, maybe. He'd learn about war that wasn't in the book, if he lived long enough to get to the flats. Lucey now figured they all would make it. He walked softly.

THE DAY OF SAINT ANDREW

This tale begins of a hot August day, and 'tis the tale of Molly Pritchard and Tommy Laing and Rob Ferguson—and, too, is Ardie MacLaren in it. Ardie MacLaren, being a good Scot, knew that the day of St. Andrew was a day to pipe and eat the haggis, to drink of the smoky Scot's whiskey—but this is not Ardie's tale, and I begin with the crupper before the bridle, which is the wrong way to begin a tale. Let us begin at the beginning, the proper place, and the way it began was this.

This town, to give it a title greater than its worth, is called Clayville; and it sits, or sprawls, as you will, on the edge of the high lonesome, in a saddle of the hills that foretell the mountains beyond—the Rockies themselves; at the verge of a land so huge and so worthless that they measure it by the mile rather than by the acre. It was a land in the midst of many a fantastic boom, in the years of which I speak, but Clayville did not boom; it fizzled.

At one time, yes, they found the yellow magnet, the gold that makes fools of men, and for a few short months the hills were alive with men; out yonder there, you can still see the marks of their digging. But 'twas but a small streak, as gold booms go, a few pockets and crannies, and, as suddenly as they came, the thousands were gone, and only a few, the stubborn and the foolish, were left.

Stubborn, you might say for Molly Pritchard, aye, and Rob Ferguson—and Ardie MacLaren, too. And me, too, possibly, Mike Kelly, for I stuck with my little bar downstairs and a few sleeping rooms upstairs, a tavern-keeper in a small way. But foolish was Tommy Laing, for this was not his land, or his way of life, and it came near to getting the best of him.

He came in one blistering hot afternoon, afoot and foot-sore, a lathy lad with the hide of his face cooked red and blistered, and nothing on his back but a torn shirt, and nothing in his pockets but his hands. And with the unerring instinct of the unfed and uncared for, he homed on the doorstep of Molly Pritchard's place. He stepped in the door slowly, opening the screen and keeping one hand on it, ready to leave again.

Molly spotted him and said briskly: "Come in or go out, but the screen was put there to keep out the flies."

He flushed, a painful thing, under the sunburn and the blisters, and he swallowed three times before he spoke. "Is there . . . ," he said in a husky voice, "is there anything for a man to do for a meal?"

We looked. We all looked, for it had been many a day since a man had come to Clayville in need of a hand-out. And when we looked, the fire sprang up deeper and redder under the baked hide of him.

And 'twas Molly, bless her heart, who had the answer on her tongue. "The very man," she said, "that I've been looking for. My chore boy's gone, and there's not enough wood in the box to fry an egg." And all the time, she was loading a plate from the pots on the stove. "Sit here," she said, "and dig into this. Then I'll show you the chopping block."

'Twas only natural that we watched him, from the corners of our eyes, and 'twas only natural that he watched Molly. Not that he let it interfere with his eating. He went through the beef and praties and string beans at a gait that showed his hunger, but for all he was watching her while she worked, he did not take his eyes from his plate when she stopped to fill his coffee mug again.

"Thank you," he said very softly, apparently to the potatoes, for it was at them that he was looking. Then, when she turned back to her work, his eyes followed her again.

A fine figure of a woman, Molly, and 'twas not at all surprising he should watch her. There were not many white women in this land those days, and none at all like Molly. Middling tall, she was, and well-rounded here and there, and with the hair piled on her head black enough to put a crow's wing to shame, and the eyes of her blue enough to mind one of the sky as first you see it at sunrise. Aye, there's been men ride a hundred miles to eat her pie and sit and gaze at her with great calf eyes, but still the fine, hard-working hands of her were free of rings, for she was as proud as she was tall, and as independent as she was beautiful.

They'd made their try, and had their say, and never a one had she looked upon twice, unless it be Rob Ferguson. Which, you might say, is not more than right, for Rob was a man to look upon twice. Tall, he was, with shoulders as broad as a door, and a grin wide and white and reckless, and a dashing figure he made, with his big hat with the curl to the brim, and the narrow hips of him swung around with the heavy cartridge belt, and the big walnut-butted gun slapping on his flat thigh. He had a pride of his own, had Rob Ferguson, and no humility in it; and he had made his mind to it that Molly should wed him or no other.

So it was that Rob took this day to ride up from the rangelands, and he came in out of the sun and flashed his wide grin on Molly, and cuffed his big hat back from his forehead.

"Hello, boys," he said to all of us, and—"Hello, sweetheart."—to Molly.

She did but give him a nod, and set out eating tools and a cup of coffee for him.

"What will you have?" she asked him.

"Anything, sweetheart," he replied, smiling up at her. "If

your hands made it, it will be good."

"I am no sweetheart of yours," she replied tartly, and she took away the hand he was reaching for. It was then that the lathy young one she had fed spoke up.

"Miss," he said, "if you will show me what you want done, I'll pay for my meal."

He flushed again, as his words brought our eyes back to him, and Rob Ferguson in particular straightened up and looked him over carefully.

"Out here," said Molly quickly, and she led him out to the back door. He nodded as she pointed and spoke, and went outside. Then we could hear the snoring of the bucksaw on the pine poles of the woodpile.

Rob looked at her as she came back, and there was a puzzlement in his eyes. "You're feeding tramps now?"

Molly retorted almost sharply: "The man was hungry, and there's no wood cut."

"He's a tramp," said Rob.

"He was hungry," Molly retorted. Then she looked at Rob carefully. "You've never been hungry, have you, Rob?"

"No," he said, "and I never will be. And if I was, I'd take what I had to have before I'd beg."

Molly had something in her voice then that made me look up from my pie. "Yes," she said slowly, "I suppose you would."

I heard the axe chunk in the wood outside, and then it made a ringing sound, and the lad outside made a muffled cry. Molly looked, then said—"Holy Mother."—snatched open the screen, and ran outside. Rob and I were right behind.

The lad sat on the ground, with both hands clasped on the calf of his leg, and blood ran down his shin and dripped on the ground. Under the sunburn, he was a sickly white, and he had his teeth clipped tightly together. Molly took one look, then pushed Rob and me apart as she went between us in haste, and then she was back with a bottle and clean rags.

It wasn't so bad. He had but set the corner of the blade into his shin, and in the meat only, without hitting the bone. He made not a sound, as Molly doused his wound with witch hazel and bound it with clean, white cloth. But his eyes were on her, like those of a hurt hound, and, when she was done, he gave her a smile with his heart in it and a soft-voiced: "Thank you."

Rob saw that, I suppose, for he made a great snort, and snatched up the axe. He set up a chunk of the pine pole the lad had sawed off, twelve inches long and ten inches through, and he grunted as he swung the axe. The blade rang, and the block fell apart, halved with the one lick. Two more quartered it.

The lad struggled to his feet. "That's my job," he said, and put out a hand for the axe. Rob gave him a sort of smile that had no gentleness in it.

"You've been fed," he said. "Move on. Hit the road, tramp. This is a man's work." Again he grunted, and the axe rang, and two halves of a block popped apart.

For an instant, the lad straightened, and a fire came in his eyes. Then he looked at me, and at Molly, and it was a pain to look at the hurt in his eyes. "Thank you again," he said stiffly to Molly, and he turned and limped past us.

Something—and I'll never know what—made me follow him. You see them all, in my trade, the bums and the tramps and the braggarts; and this lad was none of them. Down on his luck, most certainly, and he'd been kicked, and kicked hard, somewhere along the line. But curse the daft Irish heart of me, there was something in the lad I took to. I mind the time I was twenty years old, and broke, and in a strange land.

I came behind him, and I said: "Where do you go now, lad?"

He looked around at me. Sandy hair, he had, in need of cutting, and eyes as brown as a spaniel's. He nodded down the road. "That way, I guess," he said.

There was nothing that way, not for fifty miles, but one shack of a stage station, and so I told him. "You'd not make it afoot, with that leg, lad," I told him. Then inspiration struck me. "Will you work?" I asked.

His chin came up, and his brown eyes looked at me fair and square. "I don't usually beg for my meals," he said.

"Fine," I said. "I'll need a man for a few days to swamp out in my place . . . and straighten up. Your board and your bed, and a dollar a day."

He looked at me, and I had a time to meet his eye. But it was no lie I told. It took a man to do the job, and, while I had been doing it myself, 'tis a devil of a job that a man can't quit, especially if it's his own.

"Thank you," he said. "My name is Tommy Laing, Mister . . . ?"

"Kelly," I said. "And my friends call me Mike. Mister Kelly was my father, God rest him."

So Tommy Laing worked for me. He ate his meals at Molly Pritchard's, and he slept upstairs in my place. And in three days he was gone, lost, foundered completely. He'd sit, with his food untouched, following Molly with his eyes, until she looked at him, and then he'd eat as if he were starving. And she—well, I have, thank the good Lord, got age enough on me to admit I know nothing of how a woman's mind works, but she, who'd had men throw her own weight in gold at her feet, she who'd had suitors like Rob Ferguson now, with his fine herds and his big house, she took to this thin lath of a lad, with the split shirt on his back and nothing in his pockets but his hands.

Maybe 'twas the mother that is in all women, maybe 'twas the way his love of her straightened his back while her good food put meat on his bones. Maybe 'twas the worship he gave her instead of the demanding she'd got from other men; but whatever, the third evening he was in Clayville, she walked with him in the evening, and she took his arm—she that had once put a fork deeply into the hand of Rob Ferguson when he reached for her.

And Rob Ferguson it was that waited at the door, when they came back from their walk. He got up from the squared block step—I could see this from my own door—and he came forward to meet them, tramping tall and solid and confident in his tight, high-heeled boots. His spurs made a little ringing as he stopped before them.

"I don't like this, Molly," he said.

She tossed her black head. "Like it or not," she said, "it is none of your business."

"I'll make it my business," he retorted, and the whole, headstrong, reckless soul of the man was in the words. "You're mine, Molly, and no one else will have you." His hand went out and caught hers, and he brought her up close with just one easy turn of his wrist. "No one, Molly," he said, and there was nothing of humor in his wide, white smile.

Molly pulled back, without a word, and he brought her to him again, easily, with just the grip of his one hand.

Then Tommy Laing said very quietly and clearly: "Let her go, man."

I think Rob had been waiting for that. For he did let her go, and he moved in on Tommy. 'Twas sheer murder. They stood almost of a height, but there were the shoulders of Rob Ferguson, door-wide and bull-strong, and the big, rope-burned hands of him, hard as oak knots, and Tommy Laing had not the slightest chance.

He went down at the first blow, clear to his knees in the dust, and it was with these two hands I had to hang onto my own door frame to keep myself back and out of it. But 'twas years gone since I learned that every man must fight his own battles, and that 'tis better that a man learn he can be whipped, than to be propped up by another.

'Twas sheer murder, as I said. Tommy got up, and walked into Rob, and Rob's big fist made a meaty sound on the lad's face, and down he went again. But again he came in, a plucked sparrow against a hawk, and Rob, the white teeth of him shining against the darkness of his skin in the dusk, did all but hammer him to death. It took him time, minutes, but when he was done, Tommy was in the dust, plastered with it, blind and still feebly trying—but he could not get up.

'Twas then that Rob turned back to Molly, standing with her face white as linen, but making no cry. His teeth flashed again in the dusk.

"No one, Molly," he said. "You understand? No one."

Then he tramped to his big horse, swung up, and rode out.

And now it was that Ardie MacLaren came into town, striding down the street with his small, gray pack beast behind to find Molly and me getting Tommy Laing to his feet to lead him to my place.

A true Scot, Ardie, a man of more years than my own, with high bones to his cheeks, somewhat as an Indian, but with eyes of a gray-green and a sandy-brown beard that grows stiff and every which way, like the muzzle of a terrier. An old friend, for he and I came to the high lonesome with the first, and, foolish or stubborn, we both stuck, and 'tis generally a high time we have when he comes in out of the hills. But this time I was full with my own concerns and anger, and 'twas a short greeting I gave him.

He looked now at the face of Tommy Laing, and he made clicking sounds with his tongue against his teeth. He gave Molly his terrier's smile, for they were old friends, too, and he put her gently aside and took Tommy's other arm.

Together we got him into my place, and washed him off and patched him up. Then, when I'd got two good belts of whiskey into him, he slept, and we left him with Molly while I broke out a bottle for Ardie and myself.

I told Ardie all I knew of this thing, and I'd no more than finished with the tale of the beating than Molly came down. Her face was white still, and she'd cried, for the marks were in her eyes yet, but worst of all, the pride was gone from her straight shoulders.

"Mike," she said, "what will I do?"

I said: "If you love the lad, marry him, of course. What else is more sensible?"

She gave me a smile that had a tremble in the corners of it, and she said: "Rob would kill him."

I tell you, it jarred me, the way she said it. Then I thought on it, and I knew it was true. Rob would do it. Heedless he was, and bull-headed, and he'd never been humbled; and with my own ears I'd heard him say there'd be no other man have her. And with a dismal, sick sinking in my stomach, I knew how he'd meant it.

Then Ardie said in his burring rumble: "I'd hate to see ye go, Molly, but ye could marry the lad and go. Or go and marry afterward."

"He'd follow," she said. "Rob would follow. He'd drive us before him." She shook her head. "And Tommy wouldn't run. You saw him. You know he'd never run."

Nor would he. Not a lad that kept getting back up, to walk into the beating he'd been getting from Rob. No, like a blind, stubborn fool, he'd fight. He'd hang a gun on him and go to meet Rob, and that would be the end of it. For the gun was part of Rob, and he drew and shot as naturally and easily as pointing his finger.

So 'twas Ardie MacLaren and me, sitting with the bottle betwixt us, hard-pressed for ideas, wishing, each of us, that there was some way to take this on our own backs, for the pair of us had stood behind Molly this long time now, since her father, God rest him, had died of the pneumonia when Molly was but fifteen, and her with no kin left in this world. She'd baked pies in a tent then, and with hundreds of the diggers lined up to buy them as they came from the oven. We'd staked her to the eating place that she had now, and every cent of it had she paid us back. I had to think to be sure, but it was so. She was but nineteen now, and already a woman who had seen sorrow and trouble enough for twice her years.

'Twas Ardie, bless the rough Scot's heart of him, who come up with the thought.

"And what," he inquired, "should be wr-rong wi' the lad helpin' me wi' my diggin's? I've need of an extra pair of hands, and mayhap the lad'll not get rich . . . he'll make a stake . . . and mor-re impor-rtant, he'll be awa' fr-rom yon R-rob."

"And away from me, too," cried Molly.

"Would ye have a dead husband or a live lover-r?" demanded Ardie.

Molly looked down at her hands. "I don't think he would go," she said.

Ardie ran his clawed fingers through the sandy spikes of his whiskers. "Wi' the three of us to per-rsuade him," he said, "I think per-rhaps he might."

And so it was. Ardie, for all his grumbling burr of a voice, could take the coat off the back of a bear, and as for me, 'twas said my own father did kiss the Blarney stone, and some say it has come to me by natural descent. But the capper was when Molly leaned down and kissed softly one of the small places on the face of him that Rob's fists hadn't marked. "Please, Tommy," she said, and that was the end of it.

When Ardie went back to his diggings, Tommy went with him.

'Twas reluctantly, and why not? Who'd like the thought of leaving behind the one girl he loved? And who likes the thought of running away? Tommy was no fool, and, while he did concede that Ardie could use another pair of hands, he must have known what we were doing. But he went.

Which left us about as we were before, save now there was seldom a smile on Molly's face, and hers were lips meant for smiling. The eyes of her were blue still, but the dull blue of dusk, with no light of promise in them, none of the sunrise blue that they should have had.

And Rob Ferguson? He made his trips, for he was a man with a will of iron, and it was not his way to take "no" for an answer to anything. But he got his "no" from Molly and, of-tener, a chilly silence that was more than "no," and the iron came out in the man where all could see it.

He came, ever and again, and little by little the coldness he met began to show on him, and he had a trick now of peering at a man from under his dark brows in a way to mind you of a sullen grizzly, a feeling that it was only a careless indifference that kept him from a killing charge. Like a short-fused stick of dynamite, he was, touchy and unpredictable, with only a thread of smoke and a faint spattering of fire to show how close the explosion was.

So the last of August went by, and September. The sun stole farther south with every giant swing overhead, and the bucks began to polish their antlers in the scrub. October came and went, and the sharp wind began to whet itself on the cold rocks, and the town was filling up with the scattering of miners that still sought their fortunes out in the creeks.

The great flights of geese went by, their distinct crying the lonesomest sound in the world, and on the third day of November the snow came, thick and white and blinding, and, when it stopped, there was a foot of it on the streets, and the mountains were hulking giants under their winter quilts. Rob Ferguson rode in that day, his big black horse breaking trail all the way from the valley.

Most of the day he drank, and in my place, he giving and getting nothing but the barest civility of a nod. In the afternoon, he went to Molly's, and sat on a stool, drinking her coffee, and staring at her with a dull concentration.

Spring is the time for mating for most of the animals, but I'm thinking 'tis different with men. For 'tis with the coming of winter that a man needs a woman, for autumn is a lonely time, and winter a sullen. Man fights winter, or endures it, for it is like death, or a long sleep, and surely, if ever a man need companionship and love, it be in the winter.

Maybe this it was, that brought Rob back and back. Once, and sometimes twice a week, he plowed the drifts in Clayville, hopeless although it was, and his temper grew rougher, and his eyes duller, but with the creeping fire behind them. He had a way of staring at every man in turn, when he went to Molly's, staring at them with a steady, stolid glare that made men drop their eyes before his, and somehow shiver in the warmth of the room. Even the little thread of smoke was gone from the fuse now, and none of us knew when the blow-up might come.

And so it stood when the thirtieth day of November came around. It had not snowed for three days then, but it had been freezing to split the rocks, and the snow squeaked and squealed under a man's boots, when he walked. The air was so clear and cold that Old Buckhorn loomed up not a rifle-shot away, instead of the twenty miles it is, and it was on the frosty crimp of the air that we first heard the skirling of the pipes.

It brought us all out, and 'twas a sight to see. Almost in the nature of a parade, you could say. For 'twas Ardie MacLaren, and he piping fit to burst his lungs. He wore the kilt, and the bare, bony knees of him flashed in the frosty light. The goat-skin sporran flipped and bobbed against his thighs, and the plaid was caught up high on his chest with a great silver clasp, and streamed out behind, when the wind caught hold of it.

Over his shoulder was thrust up the great, two-handed helve of his claymore, the great sword of the Highlands, and the pipes fanned out like fingers, chanter and drones, the bag tucked under his arm. He was pacing off the measure of the tune, and the snow squeaked and groaned underfoot. Then Molly came flying out, still in her apron, but 'twas not Ardie she headed for, but the man behind, Tommy Laing, with sandy whiskers on his jaws and felted pacs on his feet, leading the gray pack beast.

She ran into his open arms, and she cried, and she laughed, and kissed whiskers and face with no particular favoritism. 'Twas a fine thing to see, for all the cold of the wind made me water at the eyes and blow the nose of me like a fish horn. 'Twas the same Tommy came out from under the whiskers. Thin still, and with eyes like a spaniel, but brown of the hide now, and filled out a lot in the shoulders, and with hands wide and hard from his labor.

Aye, 'twas a fine afternoon we had that Saint Andrew's Day. And didn't Ardie MacLaren but strut and pipe and drink Scot's whiskey as if it were his own son that sat at the one table in the back of the room, and him holding the hand of Molly Pritchard, and her with stars shining in the blue eyes that held the promise of a new day? Aye, 'twas a wonderful afternoon we had, even if there was no haggis for Ardie, being that we had clean forgot the day, and there was not a goat or lamb within twenty miles of the place.

But Ardie made up for it with Molly's good beef stew, with the crannies filled in with smoky Scot's, and, faith to tell, 'twas not even Ardie was sure what tune his fingers flicked out on the chanter by the time dusk fell.

'Twas the sudden silence that fell on the room that warned me. Something sent a chill breath around the room, and the dying pipes of Ardie sent a sad, off-key wail through our ears.

So, 'twas Rob Ferguson. He stood just inside the door, with two of his men at his back, and the set of his face was a fearful thing to see. The dullness was gone from his eyes, and the little flickering fires inside were plain to see.

He came across the floor, like a great cat despite the size of him and the high-heeled boots he wore, and his silver spurs made a little clinking to each footfall. A thin smile was on his lips, and the white teeth of him made a little glinting in the light. His right hand was carried wide and stiff, alongside the blunt curve his gun butt made under his thrown-back coat.

He stopped, and made no sound, nor needed to, for murder was in the eyes of him, flicking like a whip betwixt the two of them, Molly and Tommy. Then he said, in sort of a brittle, singing tone: "Come here, Molly."

"I will not," she said, and her face was white as the snow outside.

"I'll kill him, then," he said, and he reached for her, for she stood partly shielding Tommy with her own body. She moved back, and he grabbed again, and got her sleeve, and jerked it half from her arm.

Tommy hit him then, a foolhardy thing, for 'twas like striking a light in a powder house. 'Twas the flame in the fuse, and Rob with the gun on his thigh, and two of his kind at his back. Rob's teeth flashed in the light, and his hand struck for the gun; and there came a screech as Ardie whipped the claymore from its sheath on his back, and a smack as he struck with the flat of the three-foot blade. Rob's hand was knocked aside, and he half turned, holding the numbed fist with the other hand, and he made a terrible sound in his throat.

Then the claymore licked out again, and the point went 'twixt belt and body, and Ardie bore down on the helve and up on the point. The gun belt fell away from Rob's body, cut clean in two, even as he made a grab for it.

Then Ardie was wheeling away, with the screaming battle cry of the Highlands, and the gleaming arm-long blade of the claymore came sweeping around at the two of Rob's men. 'Tis a fearsome weapon, the claymore of the Clans, broad and heavy and keen with a two-handed grip that a man may swing it as an axe, and the men of Rob Ferguson leaped back before it, for the fear of the sword is older than the fear of the gun.

"All r-r-right, Tommy," roared Ardie, and the claymore swung lazily to and fro before the throats of the Ferguson men, " 'tis yer-r own fight, lad!"

Bloody murder it was this time again. Nothing barred, and no quarter asked. The plucked sparrow against the hawk, for all the sparrow was a better bird than the last time. Twice did Tommy Laing go down, and twice did he get up. Then his own hard fist smashed on the nose of Rob Ferguson, and Rob was staggered. Like a fiend's, his face was, as he went back to the blow, and then he made a snatch for the gun lying on the floor.

But, if the sparrow be small, so is he quick. He caught Rob with his fist, as Rob's face was bending down, and Rob went back and down. I think 'twas the first time another man had ever felled him. Something showed in his face as he fell.

He did not get set again. For it was Tommy carried the fight now, with the memory of his past beating, and the spur of a man fighting for his mate driving him in. 'Twas thin steel meeting iron, and the iron in the soul of Rob Ferguson was brittle, and it broke; and, when it did, he was something less than a man. Four times he went down, and then he would not get up. He could have, but he would not. He knelt there, with his hands braced on the floor before him, the bloody face of him looking at the floor, and he took his wind in great, sobbing gulps.

Then Tommy Laing was saying, gasping the words with his own hard-caught breath: "Rob, do you hear me?"

Twice he had to ask it before Rob Ferguson nodded his beaten head.

Then Tommy said: "You'll ride out of here, Rob Ferguson. Ride out, and don't come back. Do you hear me?"

Rob nodded the bowed head of him, and he did not look up. Tommy demanded again, implacably: "Do you hear me, Rob?"

Rob looked up then, and the broken iron grated in his voice. "You win," he said. "You win." Even in defeat, Rob had to have it seem that he conceded, that there might still be doubt as to the winner; and Tommy left him that little sop to his pride.

Then did Ardie MacLaren lower the claymore, and bring the flat of it across his thigh till the blade sang again. He saluted the ceiling with the ringing blade, and then it screeched back into the sheath on his back.

'Twas a dead silence that followed the leaving of Rob and his men, for who can look upon a beaten cur save with sickness? Then Ardie picked up the pipes again, and puffed up the bag so that the drones made the room ring. He fingered the chanter, and Bonnie Prince Charlie made the place gay again. Ardie looked at me, and signaled with his eyes, and sure 'twas Tommy and Molly, in the circle of each other's arms, and the world gone from their sight. I jerked my head at him, and he nodded, and we paraded out, all of us, and I shut the door behind me.

To my place we went, to the skirling of the pipes, and our high-stepping feet sent a squeaking beat out through the brightness of the frosty night. Aye, that was a fine night, that long-ago night of Saint Andrew.

THE PIONEERS

There was this steady, hurting, hammering thud inside his skull every time his heart beat. It hurt worse than anything he could remember, and deep down in the secret places of his mind he wanted to get away from it, to slide back into the soothing, unhurting dark. But his heartbeat smashed at the splintering bones of his skull until he opened his eyes to see the brown faces hovering over him.

He came up at them, fighting with an animal-like clawing and roaring, but the strong brown hands caught and pinned him before he could do any damage. Then slowly the man inside came through the fear and hurt, and he knew who he was and where. He was Byron Martin, and the brown faces weren't the Indians—they were Mexican muleteers.

The *caporal*, in his dandy's outfit of black all trimmed in red and gold, knelt down and wiped Byron's face with a cloth and murmured something in Spanish. Byron pushed him aside and sat up, suddenly remembering. The stench of smoke was in his lungs, deep—where he couldn't get it out, the smell of things that were never meant for burning—cloth and flour and scorched meat. The horses lay where they had crashed down in the harness, one stiff and still, the other still bubbling and groaning from the Rogues' clumsy gut-shooting.

Byron got his hands and knees under him. He crawled the four feet or so to the rear wagon wheel and pulled himself up by the spokes. He started to fall, and clutched desperately at the iron rim. It was hot under his hand. He heard the *caporal*'s inquiring voice, and his own words were a mushy paste he had to force through his teeth.

"Carrying the woman down to Clayburne's," he said. "Heard the Rogues was raising up, and Clayburne's got a stout house and four growed boys. Me and the woman and the boy. I loaded up the wagon and the boy. I loaded up the wagon to carry them down. . . ." Then the thought hit him like a bullet, and he almost screamed in the man's face: "They got Ruth! They got my boy! My God, man, where are they? What have they done with them?" He turned loose of the wheel to reach despairingly at the man as if to shake the answer out of him. He lost his balance and fell to his hands and knees.

The Mexican stooped and helped him up. His skin was smooth and darkly tan, and his liquid eyes were sympathetic. *"Compadre,"* he said, "you come now."

Byron moved under the gentle support of the *caporal*'s arm, seeing the little brown *arrieros* hustling to shift packs on some of the string of mules patiently standing to the side. He'd seen them many times before. The mule trains were about the only transport to and from the valley, for the only wheel trace in the Rogue River Valley was the Applegate Trail in from the east on the Bear Creek end and on out north in the Willamette; anything south over the Siskiyous or west to the coast went mule-back or not at all.

The *caporal* had a canteen and a cloth, and he reached up to the back of Byron's head, and nearly tore it off with his first, gentle, swabbing touch. Byron groaned. The *caporal* clucked and said: "Vair close, *compadre. Bala de los indios* come one hair more . . . *poof!* . . . you are dead."

Byron endured while the *caporal* swabbed and bandaged, and put on his hat cocked well forward so it did not touch the thick pad at the back of his head. "Now," said the *caporal*, "if you weel moun' thees mule, *compadre*. . . ."

Byron understood, then. He made a lurching turn. "The woman," he said. "My boy."

The *caporal* shrugged uneasily. He gestured flamboyantly at the crowding timber that threatened to push the narrow track off into the near-dry creek bed. *"Los indios,"* he said. "Where are they? Coyotes. *Diablos.* Like wolves . . . *poof!* They are gone! You come, now. *Mañana,* with friends . . . *los soldados,* perhaps. . . ."

"No," Byron said. The fear had him by the throat. He knew if they left him here, he could not bear it, but he would not go—not without knowing.

The *caporal* studied him with his soft, sympathetic eyes. *"La mujer,"* he said. "The woman." He sighed and hunched his shoulders resignedly. "And no weapon, no nothing." He turned away and went to his mount, a sleek black mare, and came back with a long-barreled pistol. "You comprehend the *pistola, señor?* To load, bite the *cartucho* . . . cartridge . . . so. Into the *cámara* . . . chamber . . . so . . . and then the rammer . . . and again and again to five. Caps on the neeples, so. One *cámara* vacant, so the hammer has a home place. So."

Byron accepted the pistol and the box of cartridges and percussion caps numbly. He could not even say thanks. They were going to leave him. He began to tremble, and the thin, silent shrieking of fear began again, inside. The *caporal,* looking away suddenly, said softly: *"Vaya con Dios, compadre."* Then they were gone, with just the faint smell of their dust left, the rear rider touching his hat in solemn final salute from the far turn.

The silent, dismal secretiveness of the forest closed in on him, surrounded him, and no matter where he turned, he felt the silent pitiless waiting eyes of the Rogues, out there. He backed up against the wagon, between the wheels so that his back was flat against the sideboards. The pistol butt was slick and awkward in his sweating fist.

In these sickening moments he knew he was a coward. He couldn't do it. He wasn't a woodsman; the little brown devils were. They were watching him now, torturing him with silence and waiting; they had him either way. If he broke and ran for it, they'd kill him from behind. If he went into the brush after them, they'd come up through the leaves and open him up with a knife or gut-shoot him with his own rifle. The half-dry creek behind him made little sucking noises of sardonic mirth. Then a bird cried, back in the timber, and his outraged mind translated it into a woman's distant scream. He moved suddenly—without willing it, without thinking—up the slope and into the timber in a heedless rush that trampled brush and twigs underfoot.

The inner desperation drove him into a frenzy of desire to get it over with, and he cursed in a strangling voice and rushed into a thicket of brush, lashing the limber leaved branches aside with the pistol barrel. There was nothing in the brush clump. He crashed through and wheeled around, crying in a choked voice for them to come out and get it over with. He backed into a tree, and the jar against the back of his head sent him to his knees.

He was helpless as he knelt there, he knew that. He was almost blind with hurt, and he'd dropped the pistol. But the Rogues didn't come—they weren't coming. That certainty finally got through the frozen layers of his brain. They had been scared off by the mule train coming up the trail.

Slowly now, the blindness went away, and his hurt faded to a steady, thumping ache. He picked up the pistol, and with absent-mindedly careful motions he brushed it off, really looking at it for the first time. He wasn't a hand gunner. Armand Clayburne and most of the rest of the valley men carried pistols as a matter of course, and he tried to remember what he'd heard.

"They've got a helluva kick," Clayburne had said once. "Get close to your man and hold low," he'd said. "Put your sights right on his crotch and cut 'er loose. Let 'er r'ar back into a stiff wrist and you got your man. Hell with picking your spot. A Forty-Four slug hits him any place, atween the crotch and the eyebrows, he ain't goin' to bother you no more."

Byron held the pistol out now, looked down the sights. The weapon was clumsy in his hand, and the sights wavered. He got up and started to walk.

He was no woodsman. He'd come this way because the *caporal* had waved this way, vaguely. He walked, almost aimlessly, among bare-trunked pines like bronze pillars rising from their own litter of shed needles and the straggling little brush that was all that grew in their shade. He found something, finally, a long scuffed spot where the needles were turned and stirred—nothing more. It wasn't much, but a questing eagerness came on him suddenly, and he moved along in the direction of the scuffed place.

He found a little manzanita with one twig doubled back under the one above, the oval leaves showing their pale grayish underside. Something had pushed by here forcibly, and the slow, inevitable reaction of the bush hadn't gotten around to rearranging it yet. He cursed his stupid lack of skill at this. He was a farmer. He knew pasture land and corn land and potato land, and he could squeeze a lump of soil in his callused hands and predict almost to the hour when it would be ready for the plow. He could rub seed corn between his palms and bite a kernel or two and tell pretty close how many would sprout to the hill; but the brush was not his world. They called it the brush, but it wasn't. It was virgin timber, uncounted miles of it, pine and fir and cedar and others he didn't know. His own holdings made a single flea bite in this vast shaggy rug that covered this wild, raw, new Rogue River Valley and its hills. And he'd spent a year of his life hewing out that flea-bite patch.

He'd been a fool in the first place, he could see that now. But land hunger made a fool of a man. He'd been a tenant farmer in Kentucky and Ohio. Free land, they'd said, out in Oregon, for the taking. Well, it wasn't free—it is never free. The cleared bottoms were all staked, and the miners rooting in the creeks bid the prices of everything out of a poor man's reach. He and the wagon and the team all beat down so thin by two thousand miles of shoe-stringing it that the cañon passage to the Willamette was impossible. . . .

The story of my life, he thought bleakly. *Biting off more than I could chew. Bulling ahead with my eyes shut and figuring a strong back made up for a weak mind.*

He'd gotten along with the Indians, all right. Hunted with them, sometimes. Ruth was afraid of them. Inscrutable little brown men with an animal's wiry strength and an animal's unthinking cruelty, they'd bird-dogged the brush and chased deer out in front of his rifle, grunted without expression and taken their share and disappeared back into the shadowy creeks where their brush huts were. He didn't understand them—he conceded a certain respect for their wild woodsman's skills, but he didn't fear them, as Ruth did, until Tynee John's bucks rose up and burned every cabin along the creek.

For some reason they'd bypassed his shack. He'd had a hard time believing the hurried little knot of miners that came by on their way to Jacksonville to warn him. It had scared Ruth. Scared her worse than she was already. And finally, reluctantly, he'd packed up the wagon to carry her down to the Clayburnes'. They'd passed two burnings—the Wiggins and Macatee places. Ruth wouldn't look when they passed the smoldering piles.

He crossed the ridge, now, and started down the far side, mostly on hunch. Marks were so few and scattered he couldn't be sure of anything. But he kept moving. It was dark, almost, as soon as he dropped off the ridge, and by the time he reached the next creek bottom, he was wandering like a lost and blinded spirit in a tangle of ghostly, formless shapes. He drank from the creek until he was almost sick; his lips were cracked and dry. He could go no farther, and he pulled back instinctively from the creek and lay on his left side with his back against a half-rotten windfall. He crumpled his hat to soften the stub limb under his dully-aching head, thrust the pistol under his shirt against the skin, his right hand still hooked around the butt.

He came awake, fully awake, with alarm shouting, shrieking, shaking at him. It brought him sharply and alertly awake, without a muscle moving but his eyelids, and he saw the Indian. Fear ran screaming down all the fine-burning nerves of his body.

The Rogue stood on the creek bank, across from Byron. He stood like a hunched statue, harking alertly as the mountain grouse do, turning his head in tiny flirting motions to sound the wind. Then, quite suddenly, the Rogue dropped flat and started sucking water from the creek. Byron moved then, instinctively doing what he had to do without thought, picking the instant he had his man in a bind.

He slid the pistol out of his shirt and cocked it, holding the trigger back so the sear would not click. He thought he did it without sound, but as the hammer came back to full cock, the Rogue raised his head in a sudden jerk and stared straight at him. Over the sights, the Rogue's chin sat on the blade of the front sight, and his frozen features were those of a gargoyle carved in walnut, water drooling down the slack, surprised lower lip, black obsidian-chip eyes without depth or life, the only movement the tiny flare and sag of nostrils under slow, labored breath.

Byron didn't know how long they posed thus. The black eyes over the pistol's sights were almost hypnotic in their steady, unwinking stare. This one wasn't a full-grown buck. Maybe fourteen, maybe sixteen—who can tell the age of a Rogue Indian? But he had him, and they both knew it. And without thinking about it, he was dredging his mind for the few words of jargon he knew, for he knew without conscious cerebration that he was going to use this Rogue cub if he could.

"*Tillicum,*" he said. That meant friend. The Rogue stared at him with unblinking eyes. He seined his brain again. *Boston.* That was the universal word for white man. *Klooch— kloochman*—that was woman.

"*Boston kloochman?*" he said, putting the question in the tone. He pointed across the creek.

Nothing.

"God damn you," he said through his teeth. "*Kloochman . . . boston kloochman.* You see her?" Eyelids suddenly blinked across those black, bottomless eyes. What was the word for *you? Kipa? Kima?* No . . . *mika.* "*Mika . . . boston kloochman?*" He went toward the Rogue with the pistol thrust ahead, and the Indian pulled back before him as he splashed through the ankle-deep water. He came to his knees, still blinking rapidly, and Byron laid the gun on the bigger target of his belly. "Damn you," he said, "I'll kill you. You understand? *Mamook mamaloose!* Speak up, damn you!"

The Rogue was afraid. He could almost smell it. And suddenly the Rogue's mouth opened, and he said in a breathless gobble: "*Klatawa yah'wa boston kloochman.*" He pointed. "*Tyee zhon man is'kum kloochman ko'pa skookum chuck.*"

Byron cursed himself for not knowing more jargon. But it sounded as if this one knew where she was. Then the chilling thought came. *"Kloochman mamaloose?"* he demanded fiercely. "Woman dead?"

The Rogue said— *"Wake."*—and shook his head, no.

"All right," said Byron. "You take me. *Mika klatawa yah'wa. Boston kloochman. Hyak!"*

The Rogue stood up. He wore a ragged cotton shirt, and unless there was a breechclout under the flapping tails nothing else except his moccasins. A twisted rawhide cord was belted twice around his waist and tied, and a sheathed butcher knife was pushed under it. Byron took the knife, tied one end of the belt around the Rogue's wrist, and held the other.

"All right," he said, and motioned with the barrel of the pistol. *"Klatawa. Hyak!"*

The Rogue backed away to the length of the tether, then finally turned and led off into the timber. The Rogue's shuffling, almost shambling, pace was deceptively fast. Byron couldn't see the trail the Rogue seemed to be following so easily, and twice, he was sure, they had left it. But eventually some sign always turned up that even he could see. Once it was a tag of cloth, no bigger than a fingernail, which the Rogue plucked off a dry spur of manzanita. The Indian looked at it, raised it to his nostrils, and sniffed inquiringly, as an animal might, shrugged, and tossed it aside.

They crossed two more ridges, and two creeks. On one soft bank, the Rogue pointed out a flat, curved depression, the mark of a hard shoe-sole, said— *"Kloochman."*—contemptuously, as if any fool should know more than to leave as clear a marker as that. Byron prodded him on with the pistol.

The pace was tiring him, although the Indian lad seemed as fresh as ever. Byron wondered how his son had stood it, if his captors had traveled this fast. Shortly after the sun passed overhead in its nooning, he got his answer. The Rogue harked alertly at something, swinging his eyes off the trail. He paused, just the slightest hesitation, and Byron sent a quick, sweeping glance around and brought up the pistol. The Indian started on, and Byron stopped him with a twitch of the leash. "What is it?" he demanded low-voiced.

The Indian grunted something and started on, and Byron saw something wrong in the stiffness of his shoulders. He stopped him again, and searched the surrounding area carefully with his eyes. He saw the scuffed mark, off in the needles to the side, and knew he had something when the Indian reluctantly went toward it under his prodding. He found his son's body not twenty feet off the trail, carelessly hidden in the scrub brush.

Somehow it didn't make sense. The little face was so pale and expressionless that it might have been a wax doll's face. The boy lay in a sprawling, sleeping pose, his cheek against the shed leaves, and only the fact that his head was turned too far from the angle of his shoulders showed where a strong hand had broken the tender bones of his neck with one savage twist. Byron didn't touch him. He squatted there a long time, while his tired mind rejected it, refused to consider it, even.

It was an ant that broke the spell. A common little black ant that skittered up over the boy's pale cheek. Byron waited for him to reach up and brush it off, and he didn't. It was as if a red bomb had exploded in his brain. He made a screaming sound of pain and came to his feet and in one wheeling motion clubbed with the pistol at his tethered Indian.

In that instant he knew he'd waited too long. The Rogue had picked up a club, a ragged-ended limb three feet long, and he swung it in a countering blow that drove the pistol out of Byron's fingers and spinning aside.

He was scared, the Rogue. His eyes were round and his mouth was slack, and he jerked back hard on the rawhide that tethered his wrist to Byron, and yanked it free. Still on the defensive, he backed away, holding the stick poised, but Byron ignored it completely as he flung himself after him. The lad cried out something in a scared voice, threw the club at him, and then wheeled and broke for it. Byron plunged heedlessly through a stand of brush, dodged through a spindly fence of pine reproduction, before the red mist cleared, and he knew he couldn't match the Rogue at this game. He thought of the pistol, then, and he ran back. It was still there. So was the pitiful doll-body of his son.

He was trembling now, from reaction, but he moved almost calmly. He picked up the weapon and brushed it off. He thrust it into the waistband of his trousers and pulled out the tails of his shirt. With infinite but almost impersonal care, he wrapped the body in his shirt. He tore up scrub brush and little saplings until he had a bed of them. He laid his burden on them and covered it with more; it was the best he could do for now. He carefully didn't think about it. About anything.

He became aware that there were two of him somewhere along in the afternoon. The feeling came on him so sharply that he suddenly lifted his right hand and stared at it as if he had never seen it before. It was his hand, and it wasn't.

He was tired, and he had to have a drink, and he was scared—with a deep, cringing, weeping scaredness. But he was also an eager, hunting wolf who sneered and raged against the rebellion of a body that wanted to quit. His head started to ache again, and he impatiently slapped it on the side as if to teach it better. He trotted, and, when those numb, impersonal legs that wouldn't obey started to stumble, he dropped back to a walk. Then, impatiently, he drove them back to jogging again.

He crossed the last ridge at dusk. He knew it was the last one, somehow—maybe it was his ingrained husbandman's knowledge of drainage slopes. He'd never been here before, but he somehow knew that this slope led to the river. His feet fell upon a deer trail that wended easily through the timber, and he followed it.

He smelled smoke, and collapsed in his tracks. It was that instinctive. He fell on his belly, and he had the pistol in his hand. He left the trail and wormed through the brush as silently as a snake, while the scared, tired part of him marveled admiringly. With the sure attraction of a magnet to filings, he slid toward the one clump of trees that called him, although it was no different than half a hundred others on this slope.

He smelled smoke again, and his heart set up a steady drumming against his ribs. A down-curving spike of dry brush raked him from shoulder to flank, and he did not move an inch to relieve himself of the pain.

The brush thinned and dwarfed off into scrub, as it would where it was so shaded, and he caught the first warm color of the fire. Something stirred, almost within arm's reach, and he froze instantly. A rabbit peered at him from a shallow burrow in the brush roots, and then suddenly broke into a skittering, silent run away at right angles. He moved up again.

He was curiously matter-of-fact about it. He held the cocked pistol ahead and slid up to it, using the elbow as a lever, the other hand back level with his chest to raise his weight and slide it ahead.

Five of them. And Ruth. He counted them as he might count hogs in a pen, with no particular feeling one way or the other. With a queer dispassion, he knew that Ruth looked pretty bad. One braid had come loose, and she looked odd, lopsided, sort of, with one side of her hair hanging free and loose and the other still rather neatly braided.

Her dress and petticoat were ripped and torn; only one shoulder held up her petticoat, and her dress was little but a ripped rag of skirt; he wondered impersonally whether the Rogues or the brush had done that; her hands were behind her, and, as she shifted in her cramped, seated position, he could see they were tied. One of the Rogues had what looked like a couple of rabbits spitted on a stick over the fire. Another was rubbing at a heavy flintlock rifle with a rag-part of Ruth's dress, maybe. One moved away and out into the brush, and then came back. Byron could hear the river talking over there, a few hundred feet beyond the fire.

The one with the spitted rabbits pulled back the stick now, and tested them with a pinching thumb and finger. He burned himself apparently, for he shook his head disgustedly. A thought came to him, almost visibly, and he lurched up and went around the fire and thrust the stick at Ruth, close in her face. He was grinning a humorless animal grin.

She flinched back from the sizzling carcasses, and he gave a grunt and grabbed her braid and snatched her head forward while he wiped the scorching meat on her face. Byron took a deep breath, steadied his right wrist with his left hand, and shot him through the belly.

The thunderous, shocking roar of the pistol jarred him, and the double flash of cylinder and muzzle blinded him for an instant. The recoil was so rough he wondered fleetingly if the weapon had blown up on him. The Rogue he'd shot took two limber-legged steps back and sat down abruptly.

The one with the flintlock started up, and Byron's second shot took him in the right shoulder blade and spun him aside, and the flintlock went off with a bellow and a shower of fire that followed the ball six feet in the air.

Byron surged to his knees to get above the scrub brush and got his third man low in the back as he dove into the brush on the far side. He made a clean miss with his fourth bullet, and the fifth sent bark spinning off a tree, chest high, where one of them dodged. He had started running with the third shot, in a charging crouch with the pistol thrust ahead. The last Rogue, slower-witted perhaps than his fellows, cowered across the fire and scarcely moved until Byron burst out of the brush. He turned then and made a clawing scramble of it, not running or crawling, and Byron hurled the heavy handful of steel and walnut with the full sweep of his arm, and hit him across the small of his back.

The red, roaring rage was on him again, and he moved with the jerky precision of a killing machine. There was a light hand axe by the fire. He scooped it up without breaking stride, and whirled it over and down against the back of the scrambling buck's head. He caught a flash of movement as the one behind the tree made a break for it, and he hurled the axe at the movement. He heard it hit, and a scream of wordless hurt, but the brush crashed as his man kept on going.

Byron snatched up the pistol and dug into his pocket for the flat cartridge box the *caporal* had given him. He pulled the slide cover and tumbled waxed paper cartridges into his hand and methodically loaded and capped the cylinders.

The first one he'd shot through the belly was still alive. He was clawing and squirming like a crippled snake when Byron stepped over to him.

"This is for the boy," he said in a flat, even voice. "You didn't have to do that." He shot the Rogue through the head at three feet.

He stalked to Ruth without looking back. She stared up at him silently. Her face was white with shock, but there was no readable expression on it. Her head turned to follow him, like a fascinated bird's, as he knelt beside her and cut the cruelly taut, twisted rawhide that bound her wrists. Her hands fell free, and she put them in her lap and rubbed them clumsily together. Her body shook as if she were weeping, and her face was a mask of sorrow, but no tears came, and no sound.

"Ruth," he said, a ragged frightened sound.

She looked at him again, with that queer, twisted, weeping face, and he helped her up. She was shaking as if with the swamp ague, and he steadied her, and then she said in a choked crying voice: "Oh, Byron!" She pushed her face against his dirty, bare chest and rocked her forehead to and fro. "They killed him. They killed little Jimmy."

"I know," he said. "I know."

Then she collapsed against him, completely limp.

They met the mounted patrol a mile before they reached Clayburne's. Byron trudged ahead with his son's body in his arms and the pistol in his belt. Ruth came behind, carrying his rifle, with one of the Rogue's ragged shirts over her torn petticoat. And something in the way they walked and looked at the mounted men kept their questions to a minimum and their voices low.

At Clayburne's, Ruth's eyes scarcely left Byron. Even when Mrs. Clayburne came running and put her arms around her and tried to lead her into the house, she kept watching Byron over Mrs. Clayburne's plump shoulder. And not until he said—"Go along, Ruth."—did she let the woman lead her inside.

The mounted men and the Clayburnes, father and sons, formed a rough semicircle about Byron, staring at him as at one risen from the dead. He looked more like a savage than any Rogue. Two days' beard blurred his jaw, and his bandage made a dirty, bloody headband. His body, bare to the waist, was streaked with dirt and blood, and his eyes had low, smoldering coals of fire behind them.

But he said, in a voice completely dispassionate and matter-of-fact: "Armand, would you favor me with the loan of a team and wagon, or even a horse?"

"Why . . . why, sure," said Armand Clayburne. "But. . . ."

"I'm obliged," said Byron carefully. "I'd like to get along back to my place. I'd like to lay the boy away on . . . on his own land. And I'll have to look to my crops."

"You're daft, man," said Clayburne. "The Rogues. . . ."

The little coals of fire blazed up brighter behind Byron's steady eyes. "They'll never do me any more hurt than they have," he said. "If they come, I'll be there. On my own land. Behind my own walls. I'm past fearing them. If you'll hitch up the team for me? . . . I don't want to put the boy down again."

They stared at him as at some strange monster, but they got out a light wagon and hitched in a team. Byron mounted over the wheel without aid, and carefully laid the bundle on the seat beside him.

"I'll be obliged," he said, still with that careful, passionless precision, "if you'll look after the woman a bit. I'll be back, when she's up to it, and find some way to get her back to her folks."

Then Mrs. Clayburne's voice came, with a frightened note in it: "Wait, Ruth, wait!"

And Ruth came, almost running, pushing her way through the men. She still had on the ragged shirt and carried the long, caplock rifle, and she said steadily: "Byron, wait. I'm going with you."

He looked down at her from the seat. "I'm going back to the home, Ruth."

"Not alone," she said. "I'm going with you."

He stared down at her, boring at her with those strange eyes that were fiery and dead all in one; and then the stiff strictness of his face broke and softened. "Yes, Ruth," he said softly. He leaned down to give her a hand up, and she leaned the rifle between them and picked up her son's body and held it in her lap.

Byron Martin shook the reins out over the team, and the wagon creaked into motion. The mounted patrol fell in silently, respectfully, behind them, making a queer formality of this escort.

As the wagon turned out of the yard and onto the narrow track, the eldest Clayburne son said to his father: "By God, Pap, that's guts!"

And Armand Clayburne said softly: "It's more than guts, son. There goes a man. And a woman. Take a good look, son, for you'll not see many like them in a lifetime!"

The wagon creaked, a homely, comforting sound, as the Martins drove down the long road home.

A WOMAN TO BE WHIPPED

I remembered it was a nice day. Warm and sunny. The stage from Jacksonville had just gone through, the driver laying the leather to them and kicking up twice as much as necessary, when Willy-Willy came. He wasn't kicking up any real dust, because he was riding one of Malachi Laudry's old plugs. Willy Williams, his real name was, but we all called him Willy-Willy.

Willy-Willy looked a little subdued, but anything that Malachi Laudry owned or hired or begot had a sort of subdued look about it, and Willy-Willy was hired out to Malachi.

Willy-Willy looked three or four other places before he got to me, down the runway of my livery barn and out at the corral, and down the boardwalk, and finally he looked at me, and said—"Good morning, Cap."—and I said—"Good morning, Willy-Willy." and he said—"Where's Cleve?"

"I expect he'll be down with a load of posts directly," I said. "Something urgent you want to see him about?" Willy-Willy always tickled me—so solemn and serious about everything.

"Why," said Willy-Willy, "I thought I ought to tell him. Malachi Laudry is coming in with his rifle gun to shoot him."

I let the front legs of my chair down. "Now just a minute," I said.

Willy-Willy nodded twice, and his Adam's apple went up and down as he swallowed. "He said he was going to do it, and you know how Malachi is . . . if he says it, he'll do it." He swallowed and looked away from me with a shamed expression on his face. "He whipped Prudence," he said, so low-voiced it was hard to hear him. "He whipped her with a trace

67

strap, right out in the front yard, and then he went in and got his rifle gun and hitched up to come to town and shoot Cleve." He got that expression on his face again. "I . . . I loosened up the left-hand back-wheel nut on the wagon, and then I got on old Dolly here, and come in to tell Cleve. Only if he ain't here, how am I goin' to tell him?"

I sat and looked at Willy-Willy a minute. He was sort of simple, and all that, and people poked fun at him, but I had a lot of respect for him right then. It could cost him, if Malachi found out about it, and he hadn't much to gain, either way. And he'd sure told the truth in one respect, anyway. If Malachi Laudry had said he was coming in to shoot Cleve Ebnother, you could bet your last little white bean he'd do it. Or bust a gut trying.

Malachi Laudry was a man straight out of the Old Testament. Big, he was, over six feet, and wide in the shoulders, and muscled like an ox, and such things as right and wrong and justice were not debatable things with him. If a thing was not absolutely right, it was dead wrong. His justice ran to the eye-for-an-eye and tooth-for-tooth variety, and there was no argument in his mind as to the fact that the Lord helped them who helped themselves. Or that one about how the twig is bent so is the tree inclined. He didn't mouth these things or debate them; he lived them, and they were so. He never promised; whatever he said he would do, he did, and his word was better than a contract in triplicate.

So the thing to do was get Cleve out of the way till something else could be figured out. And I couldn't see any easy way out. Malachi had the right on his side . . . one way of looking at it, anyway. He'd told Cleve to stay away from Prudence. But telling Cleve to stay away from Prudence was like telling a compass not to swing north.

Ordinarily, I laugh as loud as the next one at this business of love at first sight. But I saw it happen. Prue was a barefoot girl-woman come to town with her pa, and Cleve was a tramp and a drunkard and about as worthless as they come, but something happened the first time they laid eyes on each other. Even Malachi seemed to catch a hint of it.

He'd have as soon not done business with Cleve at all, that was plain enough, but Cleve could supply the yew posts Malachi needed, cheaper than Malachi could make them himself, so Malachi made his deal and named his price, and Cleve nodded in that slow, vague way he had, while his eyes kept moving to Prue and sliding away, and then coming back.

Malachi had said in his strong, forceful voice: "Very well, then, I'll expect the first load in a week."

Cleve had just stood, looking after the wagon. Prue had turned her head once—it could have been just to toss her hair back, or it could have been to take one backward look. Cleve didn't move until the wagon was out of sight.

I've seen them come and go, here in the Mills, all kinds. Miners and speculators and grangers and sharpers and lawyers, looking for business, fat and flush, or frazzle-tailed and anxious, the good and the bad and the indifferent. Cleve Ebnother just drifted in. I found him asleep in my hay barn one morning, and he shoveled out the stables and forked down hay for the first meal he ate in this town. He could have used a haircut and a bath and a new shirt; his straight sandy-brown hair hung clear down over what was left of his collar, and his shoulder blades moved under his split shirt like sharp, budding wings. He didn't have much to say, and he wasn't clever with his hands—my regular stable boy could have done the job in half the time. I gave him two bits, and he looked at me sort of uncertainly, and said—"Well, thanks."—and looked at me again, and finally walked away. No more spirit to him than a rabbit.

A man like Malachi Laudry could afford the year he lost coming West. With his wagons and teams and tools and seeds and loose stock, he was well set up on the half section he claimed, along with the two adjoining half sections his oldest boys filed on. A parcel of rich land a mile and a half long and half a mile wide that had never felt a plow till Malachi sank his into it. A strong, simple-minded one like Willy-Willy held down a job with Malachi at five dollars a month and his keep. A drifter like Cleve Ebnother, who'd had the spirit kicked out of him some place along the line, wound up brooming sawdust in the Lucky Dog for a meal a day and the tailings of liquor left in kegs and bottles.

I don't know if he discovered whiskey there or if he'd just never got a chance at it before. But Cleve was a drunkard from the minute he took his first drink. Maybe it eased something for him. Certainly whiskey was his enemy, but it was also his only friend. More enemy than friend, though, for he lasted two weeks at the Lucky Dog. Artie Cross caught him falling-down drunk and the floor unswept one morning, and fired him.

Cleve slept it off in my barn, and it was late afternoon before he roused out of it. He was sick and shaking and hurting for a drink, and his eyes looked like somebody had rammed a couple of dirty fingers in a gob of bread dough.

He came shambling out into the stable runway, and I said: "Well now, you're a thing of beauty, aren't you?"

It didn't touch him. He didn't act as if he even heard it. He looked at me with his miseries showing through those smudged eyes and licked his lips. He said almost pleadingly: "Cap . . . ?"

"No," I said, "I won't give you a drink. Dammit, man, when are you going to straighten out? You're a drunk, and you're turning into a beggar, and there's no excuse for it."

He just stood there, working one hand with the other, giving me that sick, pleading look.

"No whiskey," I said again. "Now look. There's an axe and maul and wedges in the tool shed out back. You'll find market enough and storekeepers who haven't got time to cut their own wood. But get yourself straightened up. You haven't got many more chances."

He walked out on me. He was so sick and shaky he could hardly walk, but he went out of the runway and on down the street. I cussed him, and cussed myself for wasting my time on him, and then I went out back and cussed the horses. It didn't hurt the plugs any, but it helped my temper.

It was full dusk, when he came wobbling back. I had a lot of things to tell him yet. Among them, that he could find some place else to stink up the hay so the horses wouldn't touch it. But Cleve wasn't drunk.

One eye was swelled shut, and there was dried blood at the corner of his swollen mouth. There was a scab on one cheek and dirt plastered all over him. I found out later that he'd gone to the Lucky Dog to beg a drink, and somebody got the bright idea that there might be some fun in matching him with a hunchbacked mine mucker from Jacksonville. The hunchback was only about five feet tall, but he was built like a bull, and had the reach of a six-footer. He'd been kicked around in his time, too, but it had turned him mean. Cleve was desperate, but the hunchback was tough, and it didn't last long. The hunchback beat the living daylights out of him and threw him out into the street, with that bunch of knotheads that hang around the Lucky Dog laughing fit to kill.

Well, I helped Cleve wash up at the horse trough and doctored him with Equine Balm, and took him down to the Square Deal and fed him. He swallowed and pushed his coffee cup back and forth with his fingers, and he said without looking at me: "Cap, I'd like to borrow that axe you offered."

"Sure, anytime. You'll find it in the tool shed out back."

Cleve wasn't clever with his hands. Hanged if he didn't pretty near chop off a finger the first day he hacked up a pitchy stump for kindling to peddle. More Equine Balm, and a rag bandage.

He finally learned how to sharpen an axe, and after a while he got to be a pretty fair chopper. He had a half-dozen regular customers, and he patched up an old cart, and I let him use an old nag for its feed. When the grangers found out that the native cedar and oak posts wouldn't last in this soil, Cleve found a patch of yew timber up the cañon and sold enough posts for eating money and a three-day drunk about once a month.

That was when he saw Prudence Laudry. Malachi Laudry ordered his posts and drove off, and Cleve stood there like a goose in a thunderstorm, staring after the wagon until it was out of sight.

Prue was maybe seventeen, then, but she was small, like her mother, pretty enough, I guess, and like all the Laudry family, but Malachi, sort of quiet and backward.

The day Cleve delivered the posts, he went down to the tonsorial parlor and got himself a haircut and shave and a hot bath, and, when he came by to hitch in to his loaded cart, he was wearing a shirt with the store creases still in it.

"You going courting or peddling?" I demanded. I thought I was joshing him until he turned about four shades of purple and climbed on his own foot trying to mount the cart.

I don't suppose he and Prudence had a chance to say more than hello to each other, but he'd timed it so that he ate dinner with the Laudrys, and I gathered that he spent as much time watching Prudence as he did eating.

He came back to my place and unhitched his nag and pushed the cart over by the shed. He stood there with a hand on one of the out-of-round, patched-up wheels and said: "If I had a decent wagon, I expect I could make some real money."

"Yeah," I said dryly, "and if whiskey was wagon wheels, you'd have a yardful of them."

He wrapped his fingers around the tire and felly and gave a heave that made the old wood squeak. He stuck his chin out and said through his teeth: "I'll have 'em, Cap."

"Well," I said, not believing it a minute, "it's up to you."

"I'll have 'em." He turned half away and looked across the corral with a sort of dumb, moony look. "She's beautiful," he said so low I almost didn't hear it.

"Who is?"

"Prudence." He said it the way a convert says "heaven."

I snorted. "You go messing with that girl, and old Malachi will nail your hide to the barn door."

He wheeled on me so fast I almost took a step back. "Who said anything about messing?" he said fiercely.

I couldn't have been any more surprised if a jack rabbit pulled a gun on me. "Why," I said, "no offense. Just a manner of speaking."

He looked at me a moment, then dropped his eyes, and looked away again. After a bit he said: "Cap, what's a basket social?"

I was catching on fast, now. "Why," I said, "it's a sort of party-like. The women fix up a lunch in a basket, and they put them all together and auction them off, and, if you make the high bid, you get the basket, and the girl who fixed it up eats with you."

"Well," he said, almost relieved-sounding, "I. . . ."

"You what?"

He gave me a quick, confused look and turned away. "Nothing," he said.

But it turned out to be something. And Malachi Laudry was coming in with his big .50-caliber rife to put a stop to it once and for all.

I thought of the marshal. Then I forgot it. Ebenezer Crowder couldn't put out a fire made of two sticks floating in a tub. He looked something impressive in his derby hat and flowered velvet vest with that little pearl-handled pistol sagging in the lower pocket, but he was hollow inside. If Malachi Laudry put that cold eye on him, Ebenezer would turn and walk off. And if he looked back and Malachi was still watching, he'd likely keep walking right on south over the Siskiyous.

Jacksonville was the county seat, but Cleve would be dead and buried before we got the sheriff or a deputy from there. Or I could get my old Wells Fargo out of the bottom drawer and maybe pick my spot and disarm Malachi before he could do any harm. I didn't quite believe that one, either. I could get the drop on him, maybe, but, when it came right down to it, I'd have to kill him to stop him. Not my fault or his. It's just the way Malachi Laudry was made.

Dammit, I didn't want to see it happen. I'd seen something make a man out of a whipped dog. That something was Prudence Laudry.

They held the basket social out in the open up the creek a ways above the mill, to raise money for the church. The Laudrys came—everybody came. Cleve was shaved and combed and clean, and he looked like somebody had lit a candle inside him when Prudence Laudry got down out of the wagon. A month ago she'd have jumped down, barefooted and short-skirted, careless as any boy, but the thing had happened to her, too. She had a new calico dress, long—to her ankles—and she'd done something with her hair. This dress didn't fit like any sack, either—you could see plain enough that she was seventeen and a woman. She had a basket, and there was a checkered sort of a napkin thing covering it.

Malachi went at his own steady, untroubled gait, very grave and dignified, his bass voice rolling out through his bushy beard when he greeted people. I doubt he even noticed Cleve until the bidding started. Cleve waited till they put up the basket with the checkered napkin. He was high with a bid of three dollars when he made the mistake of looking over toward Prudence. She was as pretty a girl as there was in the crowd, and, although she was trying to look as if it didn't really matter, she looked as if somebody had lit the same candle inside her.

There were a couple of miners in the bunch, flush off the creeks, and they saw a chance for some fun, and the thing began to roll. They worked the bidding up to twenty dollars, and Cleve started looking worried.

"Twenty-one," called one of the miners. He laughed and looked over at Prudence. Malachi had just caught wind of what was happening. He looked up at the basket that was being auctioned, recognized it, and then looked at the miner, a close, grim look. The miner stopped laughing and looked away.

"Twenty-two," said Cleve, and swallowed.

He wasn't looking at Malachi. People were buzzing all around and gaping fit to catch flies wholesale. The miner started to pipe up, looked over at Malachi, took another look, shut his mouth, and moved back into the crowd. The auctioneer knocked the basket down to Cleve for twenty-two dollars.

Cleve stepped up and claimed the basket, and people really buzzed. He waited, red-faced and awkward, and finally

75

Prue came forward, and Malachi was right on her heels, black as a thundercloud. Prue was looking down, and there wasn't any glow left in her.

"Will you step aside with me a moment, young man?" said Malachi. He was polite enough, but stiff as an iron bar.

People opened a path for them. Malachi loomed up big and dark and grim as death, until they were out by the Laudry wagon.

Malachi's bass rumble had carrying power. "Young man," he said, "this gathering is for the good works of the church, else I would call you to account for this spectacle. I am a fair man, but I am not a fool. You have bought your supper and the privilege of eating it in the company of my daughter. Do so. But do not come near her again. Am I understood?"

Like that. Like a prophet of old saying: "This is the law." Like a rock settling in its bed.

A month ago, a week ago, Cleve wouldn't have questioned it. He'd have hung his head and looked down and walked away. Now he looked at Prue, just one quick look, but he stood straight and looked at Malachi and said quietly: "I hope you'll change your mind, Mister Laudry."

I couldn't see real anger in Malachi. Just that implacable, rock-like steadiness. "I do not change my mind, young man. You are not fit company for my daughter. You will not come near her again. There will be no more said of it." He turned and walked away, and he did not look back.

That wasn't the end of it, of course. I suppose everyone but Malachi knew that Cleve and Prue were seeing each other. Prue's mother must have known. Cleve took on the clearing of the Porter place for what timber was on the ground. Cleve dickered with me for a team, and by the time I got around to realizing it, I found I'd bumped heads with a really sharp trader. He dickered John Sheldon out of a stout new wagon for a year's supply of wood, to be delivered in installments, and wouldn't even take a drink to clinch the deal. He delivered saw-logs to Cardwell and Hurley cheaper than they could cut and haul them. And scarcely a day went by that he didn't see Prue. The Porter place touched on the west line of Malachi Laudry's land.

Cleve earned every penny he made. He was out before daylight, and I'd hear his wagon come creaking in after dark. He thrived on it. His shoulders were wide as a door and straight as a soldier's. He was doing all right. He even had to hire a wagon and teamster to handle work he couldn't do alone. He came by, one night. He'd paid off his man for the day and finished his own work, and he said: "Cap, I've a mind to go see Malachi Laudry."

I couldn't tell whether he was looking for advice or just straightening it away in his own mind, but I told him the truth. "Malachi's a stubborn man," I said. "He doesn't change his mind at all."

"I know," he said, "but there's. . . ."

"There's what?"

"Nothing," he said.

Then Malachi caught Prue coming back to the house and demanded where she'd been, the way Willy-Willy told it. Maybe she was tired of hiding it, too. She said she'd been down to the Porter place to see Cleve.

Malachi had a length of trace leather in his hand, from repairing harness. He stared at her for a moment, and then he struck her with it, the way he'd whack a fractious horse. Prue wasn't a child any more. She was a woman in love, with a lifetime of spirit bottled up in her. She cried at him defiantly. Nobody did that to Malachi. He struck her again, and, when she would not give ground or break before him, he whipped her unmercifully. Then he went to get his rifle.

I caught Cleve, coming down the cañon. He had a load of yew posts on his wagon and his hat pushed back on his head. Two axe handles stuck out from under the seat, and Cleve was whistling and handling his team easily and capably. He gave me a grin and a remark about wasn't I lost, way up here, and then I told him Malachi was looking for him, and why.

That sobered him. Then he gave me a tight smile, took a deep breath, and said: "Well, maybe now is as good a time as any."

"You fool," I said, "get it straight. This isn't any argument. He's armed, and he's going to kill you the minute he can line his sights."

"Maybe not," said Cleve.

I was sweating. Love might have made a man out of Cleve, but it sure hadn't made him any smarter. I said: "There is no maybe about it." I hadn't wanted to, but I told Cleve how Malachi had whipped Prue. I thought it might show him what he was bucking.

He looked at me. "You're lying," he said flatly.

"No," I said. "Willy-Willy isn't bright enough to make up a lie like that."

Cleve stared at me, and he swore, a terrible, thick-throated curse, and then he kicked off the brake and smacked his surprised team across the rumps with his rein ends. The wagon went squeaking and crashing and grumbling down the rough cañon road. I yelled at him to slow down, but he paid no more attention than if I didn't exist.

We made the turn past Helman's mill, and saw them. Malachi's wagon was pulled up in front of my place. There was a woman on the seat, and I wondered for a moment before I saw it was Prue. I hadn't thought that even he would be that brutal about it. And in that one moment of wild, angry outrage I swore bitterly at myself for not having brought my pistol.

Malachi was afoot, up toward the plaza, apparently inquiring about Cleve. He had his big caplock rifle over his arm, and even alone out in the wide, dusty area he looked as big and deadly as a loose bull. Then Prue looked up, saw Cleve's wagon come jolting with the team at a trot, and she stood up and put a hand to her face. I thumped my heels against the ribs of my saddle horse and cut around back of Cleve's wagon, hoping I might be able to get to my office for the pistol before the shooting started. That was just wishful thinking.

Cleve spotted Malachi and put his team straight at him. I yelled after him, but he paid me no heed. Malachi swung around to face him and stood, legs wide apart and planted like two stumps, his rifle across his chest, not aiming it, just waiting. Perhaps thirty feet short of Malachi, Cleve reefed in on the reins, snubbed down his team, yanked on the brake, and vaulted to the ground. Malachi took two deliberate steps to the left, so as to clear the team with his fire, and leveled his rifle.

It was so short and quick and vicious it took my breath away. Cleve landed, turned quartering away from Malachi, and, as his feet bit the dirt, his broad, callused hand snatched an axe by the helve from under the seat, and in one sweeping motion he hurled it at Malachi.

It was wicked. It was Cleve's double-bitted felling axe, and he sent it in a flat, spinning disk straight at Malachi's knees. Even Malachi couldn't stand up to that thing. He leaped aside, and the spinning helve end cracked him on one kneecap and staggered him. In that same second, Cleve reached, stepped, and threw the second axe, chest high. Malachi went over backward in a desperate leap to escape it, and threw up his rifle stock as a guard. The single bit smashed against the stock, and the helve struck Malachi's clenched fist, and the rifle went off in a deep, shocking roar. And before Malachi could get purpose back into his numbed fingers, Cleve stepped into him, wrenched the weapon away from him, and brought it crashing down across the edge of the horse trough. Then he swung back on Malachi.

"Now," he said through his teeth, "you big, proud, bull-headed fool!"—and his driving fist made an oddly deadened sound against Malachi's bearded jaw and turned him half away.

He caught himself, and Cleve hit him again, and Malachi caught part of that one on one great forearm, without striking back. "I will not fight in the dirt like an animal with you," he said in his big steady voice.

Cleve said just as steadily: "You've got no choice. You've done it, and you've said it so long that you think you're God Almighty. Well, you're not. I'm as good a man as you, and, when you're down on your knees in the dirt, then you can beg pardon for laying a hand on my wife."

I'd never seen a thing touch Malachi Laudry. He was a granite rock planted in an age-old bed, and things that staggered lesser men touched him no more than rain on granite. But now he stood, and above his thick, dark beard a paleness showed through his tan, and his great bull voice held a note I'd never heard. "Wife?" he said.

"My wife," said Cleve. "With a preacher and all. But you would not give her away. You cowed her and bullied her until she was afraid of you. So your daughter is no more your daughter. She is my wife. And you'll beg her pardon, if you have to crawl with a broken neck to do it."

Malachi's hands came up and fumbled one with the other. He stared at Cleve, a piercing, probing look, and Cleve looked just as steadily back. Then Malachi's eyes slid past Cleve's shoulder. "Is it so, Daughter?" he said, and his voice was no longer big and full.

Prue came no higher than Cleve's shoulder, but she stood straight beside him. "Yes," she said. "A week ago." She looked him in the face. "Without your knowing or your blessing. Because it was the only way. Because you would never change your word or say you were wrong."

I thought for a moment she might cry, but she did not. The fires she had suffered had tempered the steel in her.

Malachi's broad shoulders sloped. I could not really read that heavy, bearded face, but his bass rumble did not sound the same. "Wife," he said.

He turned and walked to his wagon, setting his heavy boots down solidly, raising a puff of dust at every step. He walked like a blind man. He put a hand on the wheel, clenching his great fist until the knuckles stood out clear and white, and stood so, his head bowed, for a long moment while he wrestled within his soul with this thing that must be answered. Finally he spoke, without looking around.

"If you'll have it so . . . ," he said, and then he stopped and swallowed. "If you'll have it so . . . I did wrong. You have shamed me . . . I have shamed myself. I beg your pardon."

Then he mounted to the wagon seat. Prue made a soft sound and ran toward him. He loomed high on the seat, but somehow I knew he'd never sit as tall and broad as before. He looked down at Prue, and his big bass voice was almost gentle. "Go to your husband," he said. He took a deep breath. He reached out one hand and touched her brown hair. "You have my blessing," he said in that strange, low voice.

Then he reined his team out and around as Cleve reached

out and took Prue's groping hand.

Malachi rode away, straight-backed and solid, never once looking back. To me, he never looked bigger.

RED FURY

They buried Lawrence Carson up on the hill behind Jacksonville, where they'd started the new cemetery. A week after the funeral, Amanda Carson was receiving callers. A month and three days after she buried Lawrence Carson, Amanda married Todd Canfield. Back East it wouldn't have been right or proper. But this wasn't back East. This was the Rogue Valley in 1852, new and raw and wild, and no place for a lone woman.

Not that Todd Canfield was a second choice. There had been other, more persistent suitors, and Amanda could have chosen any one of a hundred if she'd wanted. Abel Porter for one—a big, smiling man of high conceit. She'd finally discouraged him with a charge of buckshot fired perilously close when he drove a loaded wagon out to her claim and made as if to move in. A week or so after, she married Todd Canfield.

Mrs. Oliver stood with the bride, and Mr. Oliver with the groom. The bride's son sat with the Oliver boys, and the oldest Oliver girl held the bride's baby daughter while the ceremony was performed in the Reverend Stubblefield's parlor that had a split-slab floor and one window of real glass that had come all the way from Ohio, wrapped in a quilt.

The Reverend Stubblefield finished saying the words, and Todd Canfield made an awkward business of collecting his first kiss from his bride. Then the reverend's wife and Mrs. Oliver hugged the bride and kissed her and cried a little, while the Oliver boys made mushy smacking sounds on the backs of their hands. Todd Canfield stood awkwardly, smiling sheepishly and red as a beet, stiff and uncomfortable with his collar buttoned up and a cravat on, in a coat too small across the shoulders, until Mr. Oliver took him out and stood him to a drink. The little boy sat with the Oliver boys and looked round-eyed and bewildered, and the baby began to cry. Amanda Carson—Mrs. Canfield now—took the baby and soothed it.

Mrs. Oliver was a hearty, brisk woman, but not without perception. "Mandy, dear," she said, "it wouldn't trouble us a mite, and we'd be glad to have them. Why don't you let the children stay with us a couple of days until . . . well, until you sort of get . . . ?"

Amanda gave her a smile, a faint, almost enigmatic curving of her lips. In her cool, gentle voice, she said: "Thank you. But they are my children. It will be all right."

At the rough plank bar, Mr. Oliver touched his glass to that of Todd Canfield and said in a spurt of words—"Luck and many happy years."—and tossed off his drink. Todd's thick neck worked against his constricting collar as he followed suit.

Half a dozen men in the place rallied in for their free drink and a chaff at Todd, Abel Porter among them. He took his drink and tossed it down, and said in a wickedly insinuating voice: "A word of advice, friend . . . watch out for that shotgun."

Todd, caught between embarrassment and the beginnings of anger, finally laughed with the rest and turned his back on the man. "This one will be my treat," he said, as was expected.

Abel Porter said: "Hear you're moving, Canfield. Shame to leave all that land when you just got it brushed out."

Someone made a shushing sound at Abel then, and jogged him with an elbow. And someone else snorted.

Todd put his glass down and said quietly: "If you've got something to say, Abel, say it."

Abel's eyes fell away, and his sly grin faded. "Well, hell," he said. "I was only. . . ."

"Then say it plain or keep your mouth shut."

Todd saw the withdrawal in the faces around him, and had a feeling he'd let his touchy sensibilities carry him too far. But he kept his eyes on Abel Porter, saw a weakly ingratiating smile come, and Abel said: "Well, now, no hard feeling intended."

"Fine," said Todd. Then he didn't know quite how to break away, and was grateful when Mr. Oliver said: "Well, best be going. A long haul back to Stewart Creek."

The wagon trundled along the narrow track. The baby girl was fretful, and Amanda held her in the crook of her arm and made soothing sounds occasionally, her expression smooth and serene. She was not a sturdy woman. She was small—slight as a girl, almost—yet she was not at all frail-looking. He eyed her sidelong from time to time, and the conviction of strangeness kept slowly creeping until he found himself almost staring. She felt that and turned her head to look at him inquiringly.

The baby girl whimpered again, and he said almost anxiously: "She's not sick, is she?"

"No. She's tired, and she's teething."

That reminded him of the boy, behind them in the wagonbed, and he turned and said: "How are you coming, buster?"

The boy gave him a round-eyed, unreadable look and said nothing. Todd took a deep breath, released it silently, and turned his attention back to his team.

The cabin was poorly built. Lawrence Carson had been ill with his final illness when he built it, and he'd likely had little skill at such things. Todd stopped the team and swung down and went around the wagon, but Amanda had descended un-aided, and was holding up her free hand to the boy in back. The boy put both his hands on hers and half stepped, half jumped, so that she caught most of his weight and, burdened as she was with the baby, staggered a bit before the boy's feet were on the ground.

Todd said: "Here now. Why not let me take care of that?"

"Oh, it's all right," she said quickly. "He's not heavy."

He tended the horses and hung the harness in the lean-to where most of his own belongings were temporarily stored. Then he walked into the cabin almost shyly, ducking his head to clear the low door frame. And suddenly, the single room was much smaller, almost oppressively so, and he felt big and hulking and awkward and completely out of his place.

Amanda was crouching down by the fireplace, blowing up a blaze from the banked ashes and coals, and he crossed the room and said: "Let me do that."

She looked up, a little flushed but still smiling politely, and said: "It is all right. Sit down, and I'll have something ready soon."

His eyes flitted around the room, fell on the broad double bed with its tufted quilt cover neatly tucked in all around, and then moved away with almost desperate haste, found a three-legged stool near the table, and he seated himself in stiff awkwardness and couldn't find an easy place to put his hands.

The fire began to thrust its tentative bright fingers up through the dry kindling in the fireplace. Todd could see the boy's eyes watching him, not fearfully, not nervously—just watching.

He thrust himself up abruptly and said in a voice too loud for the room: "I expect I'd better look to things outside."

Amanda glanced up and said: "All right. I'll call you."

There wasn't anything to look at. His tools were under cover of the lean-to, his small trunk well to the back. He sat on the harrow he'd made of poles and spikes, and filled his pipe. The land, not half cleared, lay in one short slant toward the creek and seemed to creep furtively out of sight into the brush and scrub oak. Scattering madroñas with fleshy bark and sleek green leaves loomed above the overgrown scrub of his own new claim.

She hadn't sent him away, when he came calling. When he'd come the third time and asked his question, embarrassedly daring and not quite hopeful, she'd said straightforwardly: "You've no house on your land."

"Why, it's mostly cleared, and I can have a cabin up in no time at all."

"Yes, of course, but why throw away what is here? If you could take up the land alongside . . . ?"

So he hadn't really pondered it, but made his trade and come to see her again, and, when he asked her this time, she said merely: "Yes, I will marry you, Mister Canfield."—and he had asked her to set the date.

They had set the date early, because the land had to be worked and the crops put in, and time wouldn't wait for that; he'd wanted it soon, anyway, and now quite suddenly he was married to her, and he didn't know a thing about her. He was married to a strange and remote person whom he didn't know at all, and he sat in growing dusk, shifting his pipestem from one corner of his mouth to the other, and the smoke was making his throat dry and cottony.

They ate their wedding supper almost in silence, two fat candles on the table and the dying glow from the fireplace their only light. Veal sliced thin and fried after it had been flour hammered in with the back of a heavy knife, potatoes and gravy, white bread and pale butter freshly churned.

Todd ate hungrily. Amanda spent a good deal of her meal-time feeding the baby girl gruel with a spoon, and the child was still fretting. The boy ate industriously, seldom looking up from his plate, which was a relief.

Then the dishes were washed and put away and the boy bedded in his little bunk, and the thick nervousness was back again, and a heavy, waiting silence.

Finally he said awkwardly: "Maybe I'd better. . . ."

"No," she said, as if she knew what he was going to say. "If . . . if you'll go see to the animals a bit, and then come."

He waited a full half hour before he went back; hesitating at the door and listening a moment before he pulled the latchstring with an oddly impatient, oddly reluctant hand. She had hung a quilt as a sort of partition between the double bed and the rest of the room, and she was in the bed, the quilts up close to her chin, and in the flickering light of the one candle she had left burning her eyes were enormously large and dark, and he looked at her and tried to smile, but felt it fade as her face changed expression not in the slightest. Just those dark enormous eyes looking at him from a face pale and smooth and expressionless. He looked away again, at the candle, said awkwardly—"Well. . . ."—and blew out the candle. Maybe it was a trick of the light, but it seemed to him that her eyes closed just before the light died.

He woke sluggishly and felt her lying rigidly still beside him. Then he heard the sound that had waked him, the fretful cry from the baby girl in her crib beyond the partitioning quilt, and he felt his wife stir, almost as if to rise, and then slowly relax. She was awake, he knew, and he groped and found her hand and felt its tension under his fingers, and he gave it a sleepy, reassuring pressure, and he felt its passive, unresponsive unresistance.

He pulled his hand away and lay still, feeling again that somehow something had gone wrong, a strangeness, because he didn't know this woman or her aims. He even thought with a little shock that he didn't even know her age. *Tomorrow,* he thought, as the baby's fitful cry came again, *tomorrow I'll start building another room to the cabin.* Then he drifted off to sleep again.

He built the room. It was not large—ten feet by ten feet—but it nearly doubled the size of the cabin. He brought in his trunk and his blankets and guns. He put up pegs for his hats and coats and built a closet of split cedar planks for Amanda's things. And he seldom spent an hour in six weeks inside the house without feeling himself a stranger, an outsider.

He got out his plow and broke ground, the heavy black bottom earth peeling away from the moldboard in thick rolling chunks. His supper was waiting when he put up the horses.

After he had eaten, she said: "I wonder if you would plow a garden patch for me by the house here?"

"Why," he said, with just a touch of surprise, "we can plant anything we want where I'm plowing yonder."

"I know. But I'd like a patch close to the house here. Just for my own garden."

"I'm late enough now. It will be daylight till dark for a month now to catch up as it is."

She did not argue. But as he made his second turn of the morning in the bottom land, he could see her up by the house, struggling with a shovel too big for her, trying to turn the stubborn earth by hand. She was not skillful at it, and she looked like a child trying to do a man's work. He swore a little under his breath, but kept at his own work until noon.

He went up to the house, looked at the almost ridiculously

thin strip she'd spaded, and said quietly: "There's no need. Plant what you like anywhere yonder. It's good rich soil, better than this sandy stuff. You shouldn't be working like that anyway."

She gave him her serene smile. "I don't mind."

His dinner was ready, too—hot and hearty stew she'd been simmering the whole morning in a kettle hung in the fireplace. When he had eaten, she followed him out the door and picked up her shovel.

He watched her turn two clumsy bites of earth and sighed soundlessly and went and got the team and plow. Once he looked back, and she was coming behind, carrying the little girl on one arm, stooping and picking loose rocks and roots and dropping them in a box on runners that the boy dragged manfully with a short length of rope.

When he left the field to go back to his own work, she looked at him gravely and said: "Thank you."

"It's all right," he said, not looking up from the business of checking the plow-beam clevis on the doubletree.

He finished his plowing and took the wagon into Jacksonville for the seed potatoes he'd ordered. They'd come down the cañon on muleback, and the freightage cost more than the spuds. Jacksonville had doubled its size in a month; the first scattered strikes of gold in the creeks had brought every money-hungry prospector for five hundred miles around, it seemed. Tent stores with planks and sawhorses for counters were doing a frantic business, and the street was ankle-deep dust that never quite settled under the trampling hoofs and boots. The excitement of the place was infectious, and it was almost reluctantly that he picked up Amanda and the children and started the long drive home.

Once he said: "Billy Perkins took out four hundred dollars in one day . . . can you imagine it?"

And she said almost absently: "I wonder how long he kept it. The prices!"

"Well, yes," he said, "but four hundred dollars in one day . . . !"

"There are other riches in the land," she said.

"Well, sure, I 'spect a man'd be foolish to go kiting off just at planting time." But he felt oddly restless.

They cut seed potatoes by candlelight, and he saw the small wooden tub that she set aside. "Something special?" he asked.

"I wanted to plant these in my garden," she said. "If it's all right."

He said, not quite exasperated: "I don't follow. I'm planting the whole bottom land to potatoes. Why must you . . . ?"

"I just wanted some potatoes in my garden. If you will let me have the seed."

"I don't begrudge them," he said shortly. "It just seems foolish." She did not answer. She looked down at the work at hand. And her knife winked in the candlelight.

They put in the crop. Amanda helped, dropping cut seed potatoes into the small excavations of the hills from the little box sled the boy pulled. At odd times she planted the garden plot—turnips and pumpkins and beets and parsnips and such. The crop in, Todd went to brushing on his land adjoining, long, sweaty days of labor with a brush hook and mattock and a single-bit axe. He skirted the stand of tall, clean pine. One day there'd be lumber here for a house of real sawed boards. And still he was restless.

The garden plot dried out in the summer sun, as he'd known it would, and he found her one day carrying two heavy wooden buckets of water up from the creek, her slight shoulders sagging under the heavy burden. He took them from her and carried them up to the garden.

He was amazed at the way the slight green things had come up, but he said: "I told you, it is not good ground."

"All they need is just a little water," she said.

He watched her dole out the water and then start back to the creek with the buckets, and he took a deep breath and went out to the shed and found a couple of old barrels and hammered the hoops tight against the swell of the stave and hooked up the pole float. After that he hauled two barrels of water each morning and noon and left them sitting on the float at the head of the garden, and he would see her across the wide clearing he was making, walking and stooping over her garden. Maybe that was it. *Her* garden.

The stories came floating on the wind. There were at least a thousand men in the gullies and creeks—maybe more; nobody counted them—and they were rooting out fortunes. Old Man Shively took out fifty thousand in raw yellow gold. There were others. A hundred dollars a day—five hundred— and the freighters couldn't bring their strings of mules over the Siskiyous or down from Scottsburg fast enough to supply them. Flour went to six bits, and then a dollar a pound. The sun beat down hot and merciless, and the black bottom land cracked and split into chunks hard as pavement, and the potato plants were dull and scrubby.

He dug deep and found some moisture below the crust, and he went back to his hacking at the stubborn brush. He went to town, with almost the last of his money. Flour and rice and beans, they needed, some sugar if he could get it.

The storekeeper took him out to his locked shed. "I'll tell you, Mister Canfield, flour is dear. But there's a barrel . . . the freighter had a mishap . . . his animal fell in the ford and got washed downriver, and the barrel got wetted. But you see here, when I headed it and went through the crust of wet stuff, it's pretty good." He thrust a hand into the flour and brought up a handful. "I should be getting seventy-five cents a pound for it."

Todd shook his head regretfully.

The storekeeper eyed him and said consideringly: "Well, now, you're a family man. If I sell to the miners, I'll have to weigh it and sack it in dribbles and drabs. Tell you what. Fifty dollars for the barrel as she stands."

Todd considered and mentally thumbed over the money in his pouch. "Done," he said.

"Mind now . . . it's not the best. I'd have to get ninety-five cents a pound, probably a dollar, by the time the next shipment comes, for my good flour."

"All right," said Todd. The barrel was stamped **150#** and even figuring a third loss, it wasn't too steep a price, considering.

He lifted it out of the wagon bodily, at the cabin, took the half dozen steps to the doorway, and set it down on the floor. "There," he said cheerfully, "is flour enough to last a bit."

Amanda gave him her slight smile. He unloaded the other things, and, as he came in, she was filling her flour box from the barrel. She had dipped out perhaps twenty pounds, and she looked up at him, a strangely inquiring look.

"Why did you buy this?" she asked.

"It was as near a bargain as I could get," he said.

"You'll have to take it back."

"I took it as it is," he said. "The man told me that it was wetted, but only a crust on the outside. He showed me."

She went deep with her wooden scoop and dumped it into a pan. It rattled. With the scoop tip she stirred, and grayish pebble-like lumps were stirred up.

"It was more than wetted," she said. "You'll take it back and get your money."

He said stiffly: "I am not an Indian trader. Nor you don't have to make me out a fool."

She looked at him directly then. "You are too easy," she said. "You let people push you into things."

His temper came through, and he cried: "And maybe I am! I've let a bit of a woman push me about all season!"

She gave him her steady, unreadable look and said: "There is no cause to speak like that."

"Cause enough. I've met your bargains and gone your way, and I've done everything I could to please you. I have done my best, and got a mighty thin smile for thanks. So perhaps I am easy. Isn't that what you wanted? I've plowed and planted and stayed steady and sober at it while others were out making fortunes in the mining. And now I'm ordered to go whining back and beg for my money. No, thank you, ma'am . . . I will not!"

She looked at him, stiff and unspeaking, and he stared back. She said again: "There is no cause to speak like that."

"Cause enough," he said through his teeth.

He walked past her and into the other room. He pulled down the blankets folded on the split-cedar shelf and rolled a bundle. He put in spare shirts and underwear and socks, his pipe and leather bag of tobacco. He lashed it about with twisted rawhide and picked up his rifle and cartridge pouch. When he turned around, she was in the doorway, watching him.

"Where are you going?" she asked.

He permitted himself a tight, humorless smile. "I am going," he said deliberately, "to see if I can make money enough to buy dollar flour. That seems to be the thing most important to you."

"But . . . what will we . . . ?" She was so small. Scarcely larger than a child, with something almost pathetic in the way she stood, something almost helpless and defenseless. But he remembered the garden plowing and the water and the other things.

"You'll make out," he said. "The crop is in, and there is hay cut and stacked. There is food in the house. You'll make out."

He stopped at the table in the other room long enough to divide the money in his pouch into two scrupulously even small stacks. One he put back in the pouch, and the other he left on the table. He thought he heard her catch her breath as he walked out into the dooryard, but no word came. He walked on without looking back.

The story of a thousand men had been no exaggeration. He saw that many in two weeks, he was sure. Applegate, Jackass Creek, Fools Creek, Big Bar—men came and went, stolid men, ragged men, secretive men, watchful men, who met one another on the narrow trails and along the creeks, who nodded or grunted and never took their eyes off one another in passing. It was another world, out here, a world of frantic search and dogged labor, fantastic goals and pinched horizons, a world of secretive, persistent, suspicious men, a world of icy, splashing water and stubborn, barren gravel and black, crowding timber and the thin, gray floating smoke of lonely campfires. It was a hardscrabble world, and devil take the hindmost.

Todd Canfield worked as he had never worked in his life, and had less to show for it. His beard grew thick and shaggy, and his hair hung over the collar of his split shirt. A pipe after supper was sheer luxury, and prices of boughten supplies were out of sight if you could find them at all. And time—ordinary measurements of time—did not exist. Hours and days and weeks were gone; on the creeks time was a long, endless belt marked here and there with eating and sleeping and dull, grinding labor. You didn't think; you trod the endless belt of time, and sometimes you lifted your head to peer at some nebulous promise ahead, but you never saw it, and you kept trudging at that endless belt of time.

Todd had never wanted for friends. He was an easy-going man with an easy way with other men. There wasn't time or energy for real talk. They scrabbled in the earth all the day, as long as there was strength and light to work; and then they bolted their food, and their slight talk was of luck and gold and water and sand and that elusive fortune which was likely as not in the next pan they washed. They came and went—he seldom saw the same faces ten times in succession. And he was lonely.

He thought of her, sometimes. There was a peculiar thing in his thoughts that shied off from calling her his wife or even Amanda. The thought would come from nowhere, when he was tired, dog-tired, and aching for sleep, wrapped in the one blanket he had left—he'd traded the other one to a Rogue Indian for dried fish—he would think of her body and the smooth line of her cheek as she sat at some bit of sewing or something in the candlelight; she could even make a graceful and lovely figure half crouching as she tended the fireplace.

He caught himself arguing the old arguments again, and even retreating from his own stand sometimes. Sometimes he had a feeling he'd been too abrupt, too stern with her. *Likely, now,* he thought, *it was something of habit with her, maybe. She likely thought a lot of . . . of me.* His mind delicately evaded the name of Lawrence Carson, as it shied away from the thought of love between him and her. In that mood he'd feel a little sad and lonesome, and almost sure that he'd be able to manage things without friction between them, and then he'd remember her straight, evaluating look, and smart a little with remembered shame and foolishness about that flour that had been sawed off on him. But then: *Maybe she's had her lesson by now, and would be happy to see me come.*

This was a warming thought. Then he felt the shaggy, itching beard on his face, and the split, dirty shirt on his back, and he knew he wasn't going back like that, not hangdog and frazzled, with nothing in his pockets but pride, and precious little of that. He knew now he wasn't a miner—not really—not like these men with that distant look of seeking—those to whom all save the search was less than nothing. He could not understand what goal a man might have when he dug and pried and slashed at the earth for its hidden wealth. He wanted to make his strike, yearned for it as eagerly as they, in his way, but as a means to an end, not as an end in itself. It was almost with dismay that he found himself molded into their image, growing taciturn and suspicious and narrowed in his thoughts toward that elusive goal, that tomorrow. . . .

He wasn't dreaming, when he did hit it. For a while he thought he was, but it was real enough. He ran across the boulder, deep in the creekbank, and shoveled earth and gravel from around it, and for no reason at all he labored for two solid hours with pry pole and shovel to move the thing and the nest of smaller rock embedded beyond it. Then he could get at bedrock and a pothole the size of a wash boiler. He stared incredulously at the first panning, and then he went into it like a terrier after a rat, through sedimentary sand to black sand, and for incredible minutes he scraped out prac-tically pure, coarse, water-worn gold with an iron spoon. He was shaking with a peculiar, exciting chill. He had no idea how much it was altogether—he had no balance or other weighing device—but the weight in his hands told him it was pounds rather than ounces.

He squatted on a rock by the pothole and gobbled cold

beans and venison, feeding himself with the iron spoon he'd used to scrape gold. A man came slogging down the creek, a pack on his back, a prospecting pick in his hand. He stopped where Todd had begun his diggings, and Todd thrust the food aside and picked up his rifle.

"Just keep walking," he said in a strained, unnatural voice.

The man looked up, startled, located Todd, and said hastily: "Sure, sure." He came down the opposite bank of the creek and stared curiously.

"Don't go spying!" cried Todd furiously. "Keep going! Keep going! There's plenty of creek below!"

"Sure, sure," the man said. His eyes flitted around Todd, and he grinned placatingly through his beard. "Any luck?"

"Never mind," said Todd, and then quickly: "Just colors, that's all. Just a few colors." But he kept the rifle loosely trained on the man, and the man did not stop before the threatening stare of the bore.

The hastily gobbled food lay like lead on his stomach. He tried half-heartedly to eat again after the man was gone around the next bend of the creek, gave it up, and went back at cleaning out the hole. He crammed his leather money pouch until it looked fat enough to burst. There was a mixture of black sand and gold remaining, but he hadn't the means or time to separate it. He scooped that into his cooking pot, and the silly, giggling thought came: *A potful of it. Imagine that, a potful of gold.* He found himself laughing almost hysterically.

He worked until darkness stopped him. He was tired, bone tired, but the elixir of triumph kept him nervously alert, and he heard every sound in the darkness with a hard, clear attention. He ate a chunk of cold venison, smoked a pipe, and finally made himself lie back, one fold of blanket under and the other over him, the gold fat and heavy beside him, his fingers touching the rifle. That warm picture came creeping, very real and clear, of Amanda, hurrying to greet him, her arms out toward him. He found himself smiling like a fool into the darkness.

Amanda moved about quietly at her housework, wiping the last meal's dishes dry, scrubbing the table. She moved without waste motion or haste, and then she heard the scratching sound at the door and wheeled on the sound alertly.

She saw Abel Porter's sly, insinuating smile, his bulk almost filling the doorway. "How-do, Miz Canfield," he said.

She felt the warmth of anger in her cheeks, but she said quietly: "You've no business to come sneaking like that."

"Why," he said, still smiling, "I'm just a quiet man. Deep, but quiet."

"What do you want?"

"That's no question." His smile gave the words extra meanings. "What I came for was to see if there might be anything you'd be needing."

"What would I be needing?"

"Why,"—the smile again giving double meanings—"I just thought there might be something you'd need, with your husband away and all."

She turned away from him abruptly and scrubbed at the already-clean table top. "I want nothing from you," she said.

There was silence for a moment, and then he said in a placating tone: "I thought it was no more than neighborly to drop by to see that you're all right. The Rogues are getting restless. One of the freighters had a bit of trouble coming down through the cañon yesterday. It could go hard with them for a lone woman."

She turned and gave him her level look. "I've still got my

shotgun," she said, and got her own touch of amusement out of the quick flush that stained his cheeks.

She turned away again, and suddenly he was close, too close, his heavy arm out as he stood, half leaning against the wall, so that she was penned into the narrow space between the table and the wall.

"But what," he suggested in an oddly soft voice, "if you can't get to that shotgun? Suppose you were took by surprise-like?"

She kept turning, as she came around to face him; her small elbow stabbed into his lower ribs, and she slapped him heavily across the eyes with the wet cloth in her hand; as his reaching arm came at her, she went under it and glided three running steps to the corner and picked up the gun off its pegs. She wheeled away again, and his almost blindly groping hands missed her again, and she kept the gun barrels swinging and hit him on the elbow almost hard enough to break bone; then she was clear, and she thrust the muzzles at him and eared back the heavy, curly hammers.

"Get out of here!" she cried in her clear, high voice. "Get out and don't ever come back! I will shoot you on sight the next time!"

He was stopped now, not a yard from the gaping bores of the gun, his face raw and red, his eyes almost tearful from that slapping rag, his good hand cradling the injured elbow. He said in an almost vicious whisper: "You had no call to do that."

There was a lock of hair fallen across her cheek. The gun muzzles quivered, but she could not possibly miss him at this range, and she knew it, and she said simply again: "Get out."

He fought the grin back onto his face. "You're a fool," he said. "You've made a fool of yourself all around. There's not a man in the valley would have you now."

"Not one I'd have," she said. "I've got a husband."

"No, you haven't." The bitter spitefulness came out of him in a rush. "You've had a sickly invalid and a welt-eared, bashful pup, and you twisted his neck till he ran out on you. If you'd had a real man. . . ."

In that second he knew he'd gone too far. He saw the deadly whiteness come over her face and the lifting motion of the gun and the terrible certainty in her face that she was going to shoot. He took a step back, raising his hands in a pushing gesture before his chest, and, as he saw her knuckles whiten under a clenching strain, his nerve broke, and he bolted for the door. He ran at his horse in frantic haste, and, when the animal shied away from his nervous rush, he swore thickly and snatched at the elusive reins, and, when he caught them and swung up, he instantly kicked the animal into a lunging gallop and bent low in the saddle.

Amanda stood without moving, hearing only a thick roaring in her ears. Then suddenly she was shaking, with a deep, shuddering chill, and she could not hold up the weight of the shotgun. She let it sag, muzzle first, while the chill shook her, and the certain realization that she had almost killed a man slowly took all the stiff control out of her. She started to let down the hammers of the gun, and was so weak and shaken that one almost got away from her, and only then was she conscious of the boy's anxious face, peering in through the door, and his anxious: "Mommy . . . Mommy?"

She took a steadying breath, and strength and purpose came back to her, and she was able to smile at him reassuringly.

"Mommy, what made the man scared? Did something bad scare him?"

"No, no, there wasn't anything bad to scare him. He was just hurrying. It wasn't anything."

"Well. . . ." The boy's eyes went around the close, familiar walls and gained reassurance. "I don't rike that man," he said positively. "I don't rike him at all."

"Not rike . . . like," she said automatically. "Now be my big boy and fill the wood box."

"But I just did. I filled it way up. An' I was down by the water, watching the tadpoles, and the man hollered, and then he come out scared. . . . The baby's crying."

"All right," she said. "It's all right. You go play, now, but don't go past the shed."

He went away, almost satisfied, and she hung up the gun and picked up the little girl and tried to soothe her. But her hands were still trembling, and the baby would not be soothed.

They know, she thought, *the children feel things, and know when they're not right. And when they grow up they don't feel or know, or anything. They'll lose that and learn words that can't say anything at all, and they'll be like the rest of us, stupid and blundering and rough, and not able to say things we feel, because there aren't any words for those things.* She felt the twisting of nausea in her abdomen; she'd thought she was past that; it must have been the nervousness and tension; she shifted the little girl to a more comfortable position and concentrated on calmness. The little girl cried fretfully.

Todd Canfield woke sluggishly, reluctantly. And then suddenly he had an odd feeling of wrongness, and he reached for his rifle and did not find it. Then he was awake, fully awake, and the shape that was a man against the paling, before-dawn sky said quietly: "Don't do anything foolish, friend."

Todd couldn't help being foolish. He thought of the gold and his rifle, and he shouted and reared up out of the blanket, and the man stepped in and hit him across the head in a cool, passionless violence, with the barrel of a pistol. Todd went over sideways with a great, red flare exploding in his head.

There were two of them, calm and quiet and workman-like about the whole thing, blurred shadows as anonymous as the shade whence they came, cool and competent and efficient. He tried again and was knocked down from behind—that was how he knew there were two—then they rummaged in his blanket and quite suddenly were gone, and, as soon as he realized that, he scrambled up and made a frenzied charge into the dark and smashed a knee against a boulder and went flat on his face into the frigid water and bruising gravel of the creek.

A vast and hopeless knowledge of defeat was on him; the dark moved reluctantly away before dawn's grayness—the late dawn of autumn—and suddenly he was gropingly wondering where had the frenzied, heedless months of summer gone? There was wonder at himself and why he was here; and under it all, and over, and through it, the thick, bitter poison of defeat. He sat lumpishly and stupidly while his clothing dried, looking down at the scraped bedrock where he'd made his find, his head aching and thudding to the beating of his heart.

He didn't really think out any decision. He just knew that he was all through, and went automatically about the motions of making up his light pack. Blankets and pot and spoon and knife and odd bits of leftover food, shovel and pick and pan and belt and pouch, and then he thought of his missing rifle and left everything in a careless pile while he scouted. He found it, half in the water a few hundred yards downstream, where it had been tossed in the dark.

He washed gritting sand out of the lock mechanism and snapped half a dozen caps before he could get the load fired.

The shocking roar of the piece doubled his thudding head-ache, but he patiently reloaded, went back to his pack, swung it up, and walked away without looking back.

He found a doctor's shingle, in Jacksonville, and endured while the man clipped and prodded and sewed with oiled silk, and left his prospecting kit in promise of payment. There was work in the town, and a sufficiency of busted gold-seekers to do it. Todd existed within his shell of dull defeat; he made enough to feed and bed himself at desultory jobs that came his way. He cleaned stables and trundled barrels and pitched hay to feed other men's animals; that clean, familiar odor jabbed at him in reminder that he was a farming man not at his harvest, but still numb inertia kept him where he was.

Without particular interest, he heard talk of drought and poor crops and rich gold strikes and starve-out claims and rumors of a new flouring mill to go up on the creek by the Ashland sawmill. And one day he looked up from a slogging, dirty task to see a crowd clotting like flies on carrion as a string of pack mules came jingling and thumping into the town with two freighters in bandages and a third roped stark and stiff across a mule's back.

Rogues, the boss told them in his accented speech, Rogues had jumped them, coming through the cañon north. Todd listened, feeling a vague, formless unease, and went back to work. Within an hour, other stories were going the rounds, half rumor, half truth, apparently. Miners embattled on Evans Creek. A running fight across Agate Flats. Without quite knowing why, Todd propped the manure fork in the corner, went to his ramshackle lodgings, and got his rifle.

He went at a steady, stubborn walk, bearing only the soft pad of his boots in the dust and the whisper of a breeze in the brush and the chirping of complacent, undisturbed birds, and the old, bitter defeat began to nibble at his newer urgency. He realized the figure he made: unkempt to the point of raggedness, empty-handed, save for his rifle, nothing to show for his months of dogged labor on the creeks.

He heard the creak of a wagon and the plodding of a team, and, as he stepped around the turn that hid the approaching wagon, he heard the startled lurch and thump of horses quickly reined in, and saw Matthew Oliver throwing down on him with a rifle from the high wagon seat.

He threw up his empty left hand quickly, and called: "Hold on there, Matt!"

In that instant Oliver recognized him and swung the rifle aside and cried in subdued wonder: "Todd . . . Todd Canfield! Where have you been, man?"

Todd said wryly: "Out making my fortune." Then he saw the way the wagon was loaded, and Mrs. Oliver's strained, almost-frightened face, and he demanded: "What's up, Matt?"

Matt Oliver stared at him in honest surprise and blurted: "Why, it's them damned Rogues, Todd. They're raisin' hell all through the country . . . surely you know that." His head turned quickly in a suspicious scanning of the road behind and the crowding growth on both sides.

Todd felt the thrusting urgency coming on him and crowding out the words: "How about Amanda? How about her and the boy?"

Matt Oliver stared at him, and then looked away. "Why," he said in an almost-shamed voice, "the Baker boy brought us word. The Injuns run off their stock and fired their hay, and I guess the Bakers went on down to the Lancer place and joined up to make a stronger party of it for the trip into Jacksonville. But your folks are all right, Todd. I met up with Abel Porter not an hour ago, and he went on in to get Amanda and the kids. He'll bring them out all right." Again the shamed, stubborn expression came across his face, and he did not look straight at Todd. "I'd have gone, but Abel said he'd go, and I got my own family to take care of." He did look straight at Todd then. "A man has to look out for his own family, Todd . . . you know that."

And I didn't, thought Todd, and he said aloud, not debating it: "Can you let me have some cartridges, Matt? I've got only four or five loads left for my rifle."

Matt Oliver shook his head reluctantly. "I've got no ball to fit that big bore of yours, Todd, and only a dozen or so for my own rifle. I 'spect you better come on back to Jacksonville with us and. . . ."

Impatience welled up, and Todd said curtly: "Never mind." He wheeled out and around the wagon, and took up a hurried walking gait, not looking back.

Oliver's shamed voice called out behind him: "I'd help you if I could, Todd, but I've got to get my own family!"

He did not answer. By the time he reached the next turn, he found himself going at almost a shuffling trot. He passed the turn-off—the single wagon track that led to the Oliver place—and not a quarter mile beyond, he found Abel Porter.

The body was pretty messy. He couldn't tell for sure whether they'd done it in killing him or afterward, but the body was pretty well hacked up. They'd downed his horse first, apparently; the carcass lay stiff-legged and swelling in the road. Abel hadn't made it fifty feet before they got him. Half a dozen broken, feathered shafts lay about, but the Rogues had pushed the arrows on through or cut them out to salvage the heads. Shafts and feathering they could get any time in the brush, but a strap-iron arrowhead was valuable enough to salvage, if they had the time, and they'd had time, apparently.

Todd had a feeling he was going to be sick. There was a heaving pressure in his belly, and he had to swallow hard at a thick swelling in his throat. He took that one long, sick-making look, and suddenly realized that they were coming on him from behind while he stood numbly staring, and he wheeled and swung the rifle, but there was no one there, and no sound but his own breath hissing through his teeth. He broke into a shambling run down the road, and his thudding feet drove the certainty into him in a hard, inexorable rhythm: *Too late . . . too late . . . too late.*

It was something over a mile. He'd covered maybe half of it, when the road took its downhill slant, and he could see the tower of smoke over the thinning timber. His feet lifted and fell with nightmare slowness, heavy and reluctant, and he charged heedlessly into the brush, crashing over and through it to save the precious strides the road wasted in its slow curve toward the clearing.

Then the timber was thinning, and the thick plume of smoke was out across the clearing where the sheds and haystack had been, and the hearty, phlegmatic boom of a shot came again. Then he could see the clean, sharp line of the cabin roof, still standing, and a great, choking ball of thankfulness crowded up in his chest, and he was sprinting across the new-cleared part, crouching, because some cool, sensible part of his mind said so, keeping himself covered somewhat by the dried piles of brush he'd left when he worked here last, and, when he saw his first Rogue, it was with no surprise at all—a brown, lithe figure, making a fluid, animal run from one brush pile to another and loosing an arrow at a cabin window as it ran.

Todd took one deep, steadying breath, lifted the rifle, and fired. The naked brown shoulders reared up, and the Rogue gave a hoarse, cawing yell and fell spread-eagled across the brush pile. Todd felt a giddy rush of triumphant blood to his head. There was a delightfully gritty, salty taste in his mouth.

He felt choked and short-winded, but his body moved with a wonderful ease and precision. He dug into his cartridge pouch, bit the crimped, waxed-paper end, and rammed it down the muzzle. He cocked the heavy hammer, flicked off the split, expended primer, and thumbed a bright copper cap on the nipple.

He ran at the corner of the cabin, saw a capering figure dart out from behind the blazing huddle of the shed—a small, capering figure made unreal and slightly ridiculous because it was wearing Abel Porter's ample trousers, bagging and flapping about the legs—and Todd fired again, still running, and made a clean miss. Without breaking stride, Todd bit, set, and rammed the cartridge, cocked and capped, and then he was at the corner of the cabin, and two of them, sheltered in the angle of the ell where he'd put on the new room, were wheeling on him, mouths open and yelling, one of them dropping the bar from the tool shed where he'd been prying at the window frame, and the other throwing his weight into a thick, curved bow with practiced deadly competence.

The arrow cut a short, burning streak across his arm and peeled a strip of walnut from the rifle stock as Todd fired, and the Rogue dropped the bow and stepped back and slid his back down the rough logs, hugging his belly and plowing a little furrow with each heel as he sat down stiff-legged. Todd leaped and swung the rifle barrel in a killing sweep at the other one, who dodged with animal quickness and ran; Todd hurled the empty weapon at him and hit him across the back; and then Todd was at the woodpile, and he picked the axe out of the clutter of wood without breaking stride and rushed at the one who kept snapping a rusty flintlock that wouldn't fire.

Todd was wholly savage in that moment. There was nothing human or merciful about him. His man dropped the useless gun and wheeled away, staring with frustration and fighting fury, and then Todd closed on him and swung the axe with no more compunction than if he were killing a chicken. He felt the blade bite deep and jerk free, with no more than a deep, savage satisfaction, and then he turned away, and saw the one he'd hit with the empty rifle coming up on one knee, an arrow cocked to the string. He knew he couldn't beat this one or dodge it, but strangely there was only a dull, numb regret that it had to be this way, and then a great bellow shouted across from the cabin, and a spout of cotton smoke, and the Rogue was literally lifted aside and dropped as the brutal charge of buckshot hit him no more than twenty feet from the muzzle.

As quickly as that, it was over. They were fighting men, the Rogues, but not crazy; they were little men, crudely armed, and they had no stomach to face up to this crazed giant who killed with anything that came to hand, who roared like a wounded bear and struck like lightning and killed three men quicker than one could tell about it.

Two of them picked themselves out of hiding places and ran in darting zigzags for the sheltering timber while Todd snatched at his rifle and loaded with fumbling fingers, and cursed in bitter outrage at the tools that would not do his bidding.

Then reason came back to him, slow reason percolating through the heavy, savage layers of bitter, killing anger, and he turned almost unwillingly toward the door of the cabin, seeing the splintered marks of force at its edges, smelling the deep, stinking smells of his burning possessions in the fire behind him, and then the door opened, and she was staring at him with eyes dark and enormous in a face so thin and pale it hurt him to look at it. She was holding the shotgun in her hands, and she set it aside very carefully and leaned it against the wall, and took two stiff, slow steps toward him, and then suddenly she ran that last few steps, and her head was against his chest, and she was gasping in a thin, whispering voice: "Oh, Todd . . . Todd . . . Todd!"

He had an arm across her shoulders, and he said in a strained, awkward voice: "You're all right? You're not hurt?"

"I'm all right. I'm. . . ." And then she was crying, in great, shuddering sobs, clinging to him like a frightened child, and he made aimless, soothing noises and awkward pattings, and was conscious of the dirty shirt against which her face was pressed, and the shaggy hair hanging over his ears—now when had he lost his hat? Then, as quickly as she had broken, she regained her composure, and she took a deep, shuddering breath and straightened her shoulders, under his embrace, and he reluctantly let her go.

She looked around at the doorway, quickly, almost frightenedly, and, when her eyes fell on the Rogue, propped sitting and dead in the angle of the ell, she gasped and shuddered and looked away.

"You go back inside," he said quickly. "Go inside, and I'll take care of this. Is that gun loaded?"

"Yes."

"Then take it and go inside. Keep a watch out of the windows. I don't think they'll be back, but watch anyway."

He had killed without thought or compunction, almost joyously, and now he did not want to look at the bodies or touch them. He did not hate them or feel anything about them save a reluctance that made their disposal a task he shrank from. But he dragged them, one at a time, out beyond where the shed had been, and he covered the huddled bodies decently with a charred bit of wagon cover he found by the fire and then undercut the bank until it collapsed and buried them.

Then he went back to the cabin and said through the

door—"It's all right now."—and turned back to the water barrel and dipped out a panful and started to wash himself, favoring the hurt arm that was beginning to pain him. He looked up from his splashing, and found her beside him with a towel ready. He muttered his thanks and rubbed his face and head dry.

"Are you hungry?" she asked in her quiet, practical voice.

He suddenly realized he was—enormously. He nodded.

She went back into the house, and he seated himself on the bench, drawn well out from the wall where he could watch the clearing, the rifle leaning against his thigh.

When she called him, he called back: "Bring it out here! Where I can keep a look-out!"

He ate hungrily. The boy, an inch or two taller than when he'd seen him last, came carefully, bearing a thick mug of tea in both hands. Todd grunted thanks past a mouthful of food and, feeling the awkward silence, said: "These potatoes from our crop?"

"Yes."

"Well, maybe we'll have a crop, anyway."

After a moment, she said carefully: "These are out of the garden, Todd. The crop in the bottom land failed. The ground baked as hard as brick. I dug some, and they're not much bigger than walnuts."

He looked up and then down, and said tentatively— "Well."—and then was silent. There wasn't much else to say.

Suddenly he wasn't hungry any more, and he put the dish down on the bench beside him, and sent along a close, scanning look at the full perimeter of the clearing, Amanda took his dish away. He watched her go with only part of his attention, a great depression settling over him. Full circle again. Like a cow on a tether working around a stump. He'd thought, maybe, just for a moment, when she ran to cling to him. . . .

He was aware of the small boy's steady regard, the round, wondering eyes on him. "Injuns," the boy said.

"Huh? What?" He took a quick, circling look, saw nothing, and came back. "No," he said. "They're gone."

The boy nodded solemnly. "All gone. Mommy said."

"Eh?" He put a puzzled look on the boy.

"Mommy said . . . "—with the confidence of a five-year-old—"Mommy said . . . 'Don't be scared. Todd will come. Todd won't let the Injuns hurt us. You'll see. Don't be scared.' " He moved closer and put a hand on Todd's knee. "I wasn't scared," he said stoutly. "Were you scared?"

"Well, yes," said Todd slowly, "yes, I was, a little bit."

"Well, I was, too, a little bit. But you came, like Mommy said . . . and you sure fixed those old Injuns, di'n't you? What did you do . . . put 'em in the ground, like my daddy?"

Todd found it hard to swallow suddenly. "Well, yes, something like that. Look, you'd better run along now. Go see if you can't help your . . . your mommy."

The boy turned away obediently, and then put his hand back on Todd's knee. "I rike you," he said suddenly and shyly, and then he turned and ran sturdily toward the cabin.

Todd sat quite a while, knowing he ought to be doing things. Be dark before long. Ought to check on the stock—the cow was dead, he'd seen the carcass, but he didn't know about the team or the calf. Hadn't thought, really. Well. . . .

He stood in the doorway, framing the words. "I 'spect," he said carefully, "I'd best see to getting you safe in town before I see how much I can save of the crop."

She turned on him then, her lips quivering, a note he'd never heard before crying out in her voice. "Is that all you came for, Todd?"

"Why," he said uncomfortably, "I was only thinking of you . . . and the kids."

"Then let us stay, Todd. Don't send us away. When will you sleep? How will you rest? You can't work and watch and never sleep. Why do you think I stayed? For this house? For the crop? No, Todd. I stayed because every day could be the day you came home." And quite suddenly she was crying, weeping as openly and unashamedly as a heartbroken child. "When . . . when they came, I didn't care. They came shooting and screaming and burning, and I didn't care. Oh, Todd, can't you see? If you didn't come, it just didn't matter! Oh, Todd, I've tried so hard! I've tried to be a good wife and hold up my part, and not be a burden, but I can't be strong alone . . . I just can't! I'll watch while you sleep . . . I'll work in the fields . . . but don't send me away. Todd! Please!"

He wasn't quite sure when she came to him, but he was holding her slight, strong body close and trying awkwardly to soothe her while shame and warmth and a foolish, giddy delight ran all through him. Quite suddenly he was seven feet tall and ready, willing, and able to take on the whole Rogue nation or anyone else, all together or one at a time.

He put a gentle forefinger under her chin and tipped her head up until he could look into her dark, swimming eyes. And somehow, as he said it, he knew it was more than a promise.

"Sure, now," he said, "it's all right. I'll not be going away again. Not ever."

KILLER AT LARGE

The bullet didn't sing, as some people claim they do. A ricochet has a high, whining, singing note perhaps, but a near miss by an aimed bullet makes a short, terrifying, ripping sound that is gone almost before you really hear it, and this one was a very near miss. Jim Marshall heard the sound and recognized it and yelled in alarm and reined in his horse. When the rifleman didn't show himself, Jim sensibly turned and rode back the way he'd come.

He phoned the sheriff, when he got home, and the sheriff told him if he, Jim, would sign a complaint, he, the sheriff, would send a deputy out to straighten things out.

The deputy did not straighten it out. He drove out to the suspect's shack in the west Cowhorn country. He got no reply, when he hailed the shack, or even when he went up and hammered on the door. He walked around the shack and found an illegal dressed venison hanging in the shade. About that time, a voice, the source of which was invisible to the deputy, told him that, if he was smart, he'd go away now, and the deputy later stated that the request was couched in profane and even obscene language. The deputy argued briefly, until he heard the sound of a rifle mechanism clicking, and he wasn't so much outraged as warmly irritated. He made the long drive back, and shortly after he hit Route 222 he spotted a State Patrol car and flagged it, on impulse.

Trooper Johnny McVey listened wryly and consideringly. In this state the Patrol had the added duty of enforcing game laws. This time they parked the cars half a mile below the shack and walked in, and this time the rifleman did not miss. They surveyed the shack from the last turn of the road, and

Trooper McVey stepped out. Then he threw back his head and made a startled sound. His visored cap flew off, and Johnny fell back atop it, with one leg doubled under him. He died without further sound or struggle. The soft-nosed slug had smashed completely through his head.

A second bullet plucked at the deputy's sleeve and tore bark from the sapling against which his shoulder touched. Shock or reaction sent the deputy a couple of staggering steps, and later investigation showed that the third bullet passed so neatly between his arm and body that the cloth was abraded.

The deputy fired two shots from his pistol to discourage pursuit, and ran back to the cars. From the Patrol car he got a riot gun and radioed a message. Then he retreated into the brush with the riot gun where he could watch both cars and the road. Reinforcements arrived, and the body of Trooper Johnny McVey was recovered. The shack was deserted.

The illegal venison was confiscated and the shack placed under guard. A party immediately went into the brush in an effort to locate the killer. They were unsuccessful. So went the factual and unemotional reports.

All was not so unemotional, or so factual. Police radio dispatchers enunciated clearly and flatly and passionlessly into their microphones, but these are attributes of police dispatchers. As the voices spoke mushily from car receivers, the black cars scurried bug-like through the network of highways, converging on the triangular area of Hogback, Cowhorn, and the 222 junction. A reporter phoned his preliminary story from the resort at Sapphire Lake in time for the evening edition. Valley radio stations interrupted network shows to broadcast bulletins. With a net result totaling zero. The killer had vanished without a trace.

The first week fifty tips and rumored sightings of the killer were received by the papers, radio stations, and police. Itinerant workers and casual hitchhikers learned to stand very still and without protest as state troopers and other policemen with carefully blank and watchful eyes stopped and questioned them. And by the end of the week there was other news, to take its few days of limelight, and the killer moved off the front pages. The tips and rumors dwindled. The story had gone sour until something more happened. The papers printed periodic statements issued by the State Patrol. It wasn't front page stuff, except to Bill Dawson of the *Register* upstate. He couldn't front-page the scant paragraphs he got, but he was a man with a hunch. On the tenth day, he called in Clyde Cameron and gave him the assignment, and, because that was Bill Dawson's way, he made it sound like he was cutting Clyde's throat.

Clyde said, being almost desperately reasonable and knowing it wasn't going to do a bit of good: "I'm supposed to be going on vacation tomorrow, Bill. Let's be reasonable about this."

Bill wouldn't play it that way. Bill was being the white shirt, bow-tie, hard and blasé desk man today. "So," he said, "you've practically been on vacation since you came here."

"Oh, come off that stuff. I'm serious."

"You think I ain't, Clyde? I take a country boy the likes of you, comb the hay out of your hair, starve you till I get you broke to wearing shoes, teach you to spell, teach you to run a typewriter with something besides your four thumbs, and you go moody on me. Temperamental. Going on vacation, he says. Kicking about a simple little assignment. Admit it, Clyde, you didn't know a period from a point before I took you in hand. Is this the way to treat the hand that burped you?"

"Oh, stop it," Clyde said tiredly, "before I break down and cry."

Bill looked at him coldly. "All right," he said finally, "I've tried sweet reason, and no fumble-thumbed, tripe writer of your caliber is capable of reasoning above the level of a bar stool. Now we use naked strength." He pulled open a drawer. "Where'd I put that bullwhip?" he muttered. "Ah, yes, here it is."

He came up with a fistful of column clips and yellow tele-types and tossed them on the desk. "That's where you start," he said. "This order came down from upstairs, so you might just as well stick a pair of clean socks in your hip pocket and get with it. I couldn't change it now, if I wanted, and I don't wanna, particularly. You'll be on the swindle sheet, and if you can't pay for your vacation out of that, so help me I'm going to snatch you back to covering the flower shows and ladies' club teas for visiting poets. So shuddup and listen."

Bill unfastened the sheaf of clippings and started spinning them across the desk like a practiced poker dealer. "We've milked this for about all it's worth so far, Clyde. There's nothing else coming in with any meat to it. The thing's bound to break . . . it's got to break . . . and we want somebody down there on it when it does.

"Here's the first thing we had on it. A P wire release about the county deputy who got threatened when he went to inves-tigate another reported shooting. Seems some rancher rode up too close to a poacher and drew a warning shot, and, when he reported it, the deputy who went out pretty near collected a hole in *his* hat. So he retreated and picked up a state cop, and started in again on foot. Some more cops went in and got the body that afternoon. The state cop never even got his gun out of his holster . . . shot through the head. The deputy got away.

"This was ten days ago, and, to date, the killer has simply gone up in smoke. Posses, hounds, forest service look-outs, planes, radio, everything. Not one physical trace and forty thousand rumors. Now what we want is that you get on the ball of your foot and get down there and get us a couple of features on it, working these angles. One . . . we've got the killer's name, but that's about all. Never had a picture taken apparently, or got in the papers to any extent. Family has refused to talk to reporters, and the cops have got nothing out of them but yeses and noes. It's obvious that a real reporter hasn't got in his licks yet."

"Gee, thanks, chief," said Clyde dryly.

"Don't mention it. There's hardly an honest day's work to it, anyway. All we want is a couple of pages for the Sunday feature section on the killer and his family. Ray's down there, shooting now . . . he'll back you up with pics. Two . . . we can use a tie-in with some of the same sort of stuff out of the files. Morgue will have a folder of extra clips for you to work from. A double page will do on that, too. Just some recap on that wild-man character up north . . . 'way back, but it's still good . . . ate raw meat and lived out in the woods for a couple of years. Shot two or three people. And then that sheepherder a few years back . . . went off his rocker and wiped out a family, the one that called himself the Angel of Death. And maybe that logger who got some bad ice in his prune juice and clobbered the camp with a double-bitted axe. Why, hell, man, it's a snap. We've done everything but write it for you."

"Fine, fine. Then all you've got to do is put some bright cub on it and let me get on with my vacation. I'm going over to the beach this year and just wallow in the sand and ogle the girls. I'm not even going to. . . ."

"You're going down to Sapphire Lake, and your assignment starts right now. Stop by the morgue and get that folder and stop by the cage and get your voucher, and go. Have that first feature on this desk by Wednesday. And if anything hot breaks, I want it on this desk five minutes before it happens. You goof off on me, and you'd better keep right on south. *With* your shield or on it, soldier."

Clyde bunched the clips together and shoved them into his jacket pocket where they made a bulge. "This is pretty high-handed, Bill," he said quietly.

"I told you it came from upstairs. I'm not picking on you, and I imagine they'll make it right with you if you turn in some good copy."

"Yeah, maybe they'll give me a Thursday afternoon off, if I'm all caught up."

He stood up, neither tall nor distinguished, a working newspaperman whose very name—Clyde Cameron—fit him as neatly as his coat. He was neither dapper nor rumpled, broad nor lean, and he had long ago learned that averageness could be an advantage, and that what a man had in his head was a little more important than the shape and style of the mechanism that carried it around. He had a certain facility with words, and he had learned, also, how little that meant in newspaper work, where a man's copy went through a dozen hands that trimmed, changed, rewrote or simply killed, according to the impersonal hunger of the pulp-paper sheets that went into a daily newspaper. The word facility was channeled now usually into the impersonal, anonymous statement of the obvious that is called reporting. He wrote a reasonable quota of Sunday magazine-section features, ranging from barn-lot philosophy to thumbnails of visiting celebrities and local characters. He had gone the distance from country weekly through small-town daily and county-seat daily and out-of-town correspondent for the big town papers until he stood now in the front rank of the skilled professionals who keep a big family functioning.

Bill said as Clyde started to turn away: "Maybe you'll get a chance to visit with your family while you're there."

Clyde said briefly: "Mother went to California to live with my sister after Dad died, and the other sister's in Chicago."

"But didn't your wife go down there a while . . . ?"

"Yes," said Clyde bleakly, "right after her lawyer filed. When a woman puts it in writing that she wants out . . . Bill, you haven't got a wife any more."

Bill pushed papers aimlessly on the desk and said awkwardly without looking at him: "Sorry, Clyde. I didn't know."

"That's all right," he said tonelessly.

Clyde automatically punched the wrong button in the apartment-house self-service elevator, swore silently, canceled, and punched the right one. He'd moved down a floor, into a smaller apartment, after Kathy left, and, sometimes, when he was tired or preoccupied, he punched the wrong button.

He packed two bags, checked his rod case and tackle box, put a thick folder of paper and carbon atop his portable, closed the case, and then remembered to write a note to the maid, telling her to take home what she could use of the few perishables in the refrigerator in the kitchenette and to throw out the rest.

The illuminated disk at the elevator said **IN USE**, and he waited without irritation the three or four minutes it took for it to come up to his floor. It was a matter of mild wonder to him, in moments of satisfaction, and he realized it dated back to Kathy's leaving. He hadn't been particularly hot-tempered, but delays and slowness had irritated him, and a thirty-second wait for the elevator had sent him for the stairs.

But somehow it didn't matter now—not that he was getting sweet-tempered, he admitted wryly—he just didn't give a damn. Two months ago, although he'd been a little less solvent financially and with the added responsibility of a wife, he'd probably have rebelled much more violently toward an assignment that canceled his vacation. Quite conceivably, he might have carried it to the ultimate of quitting, if the injustice of the thing had struck him so; now, with nothing in the world to keep him from quitting on a moment's notice, he accepted it with a dull indifference that put up only token automatic resistance.

The elevator finally came and opened its door for him, and he took his bags down and loaded them into his car. Automobiles were practically his only weakness, perhaps his greatest sublimation of averageness. He didn't look or act like a convertible-type man, but his car was a sleek, conservative, custom convertible coupé, mildly hopped up, and painted a lustrous black.

He took the secondary route, figuring that, if it weren't so smooth or wide, it wouldn't draw as heavy traffic, and justified his reasoning by covering over two hundred miles at moderately high speed before he stopped for lunch. It was as pleasant a time as he had spent lately. He enjoyed driving. The day was clear and warm, and the clever, competent machine functioned smoothly. He turned on his radio once, got a hillbilly type who played a guitar twangily, sang nasally and twangily, and discouraged twangily on the merits of a certain type of flour. He snapped it off and settled himself into the narrow, unthinking groove of covering ground. He had one bad moment when he saw the café sign ahead and half turned to the empty seat beside him and almost said: "That was a pretty good place to eat, wasn't it? Didn't we . . . ?" They had, a couple of times, he and Kathy, only she wasn't along this time, and she wasn't going to be, and how big a chump can you be, pal? Let's get on with it, and knock off the high school sophomore stuff, huh? But his foot went back onto the accelerator, and he drove another twenty miles before he stopped.

Sapphire Lake Resort was rustic. Which meant you paid first class hotel rates for a room done in knotty pine, and carried your own bags. The food in the dining room downstairs off the lobby was fair and the prices first class again, although the breathtaking view of the lake through the pines abated the pain somewhat. He had the chicken-in-a-basket and ice cream for dessert, and wandered out of the lodge and down to the dock, feeling just pleasantly tired from the long day's drive. A black coupé with **STATE PATROL** lettered on the door was parked by the boathouse, and a uniformed trooper, a big man, was scanning the lake with field glasses.

Clyde strolled over and introduced himself. "How is the manhunt going?" he inquired.

"You'll have to see the captain about a statement," said the trooper. He wasn't surly or rude about it, just business-like and impersonal. He turned away to stow the field glasses in the car, and Clyde saw the horizontal bar on his sleeve below the Red Cross shoulder badge. The bar had the single word **SERGEANT** stitched on it.

"Off the record, Sergeant," said Clyde. "I've no intention of broadcasting the plan of procedure."

"You're from the *Register*, you said? You'd know Ray Courtney, then."

"Sure. As a matter of fact, I'm supposed to meet him at the lodge this evening. They told me he was out shooting pictures right now."

"Yeah. Well, then, off the record, we're working on it. He's out in the brush somewhere . . . maybe behind that log over there . . . maybe clear over on the coast by now, only I don't think so. I think he's in the triangle, and he'll stay there till we flush him out."

"Triangle?"

The sergeant reached into the car and unfolded a detailed map. "Route Two-Twenty-Two runs nearly northeast-southwest, and here's Sapphire Lake. About twenty miles down here is the junction with Route Sixty-Two, with Sixty-Two wyeing off to the northwest. Now this range of mountains runs almost east and west from Whaleback to Cowhorn, about sixteen miles north and east of here. There's your triangle, about thirty-five to forty miles to the side, and not a dozen people living in it. And our boy knows it like the palm of his hand. He can stay in there till he dies of old age, if we don't root him out."

Clyde thought he caught a faint note of bitterness in this last, and he said casually without looking up from the map: "I suppose that's what you're working on now, then?"

The sergeant folded the map with quick, practiced motions and said dryly and impersonally: "Not me, mister. I'm checking those fishermen to see that they don't slip a live minnow on their hooks. That's against the law, you know."

This time Clyde was sure he caught the bitterness. "I suppose you knew the murdered patrolman?"

"From the day he went into the training academy. I was one of them that went in and got the body. I was one of the two that went to tell his wife. That's hard duty, mister. Eight years ago I was his instructor . . . school of arrest. If I hammered it into those rookies once, I did it a hundred times. Be patient, be polite, be firm, *be careful!* Eight years and two kids, and I have to go tell Peggy that some worthless pinhead has killed Johnny. Shot him down like a steer in a slaughter house. That's tough duty."

"I can imagine," said Clyde. "What about the killer? Tollifer, isn't that it?"

"That's right. Leroy Tollifer. A wild one . . . genuine ridgerunner. In and out of trouble all his life. Johnny and I both had taken him in a couple of times each."

"Ex-G. I., I understand."

"That's right, but he didn't learn his meanness in the Army. They had to come and get him when they called his number. I heard he was in trouble in the service, too. Understand he did all right in combat. He would. He's a crack shot, and he'd have plenty of live targets."

"Yeah. Well, thanks, Sergeant . . . what is your name, by the way?"

"Lawe. J. J. Lawe."

Clyde grinned. "No! You're not the . . . sure, I've seen your name before. John Lawe, of the State Patrol. Glad to meet you."

The sergeant said stiffly: "I'm getting a little tired of some reporter doing a funny story on my name every time I give a speeder a ticket. And like I said, what we just talked about is off the record. You see the captain if you want a statement."

"Maybe we could form a club. You've got no idea what the humorists can do to a name like Clyde. It's off the record. I'm supposed to do a feature on the killer and his family, so if I wanted to use anything you've told me about him, you won't be quoted. It'll just be dope I picked up."

"O K," said the sergeant.

He got into his car and drove off around the boathouse, and Clyde saw the dust rising as he drove the dirt road that circled toward the end of the lake. Clyde turned back toward the lodge. The far shore of the lake was almost invisible in the dusk, and only Cowhorn Peak held the last golden touch of day.

There was a bingo game going in the big recreation room off the lobby, and Clyde looked in there without spotting Ray Courtney, and he went on into the dining room and found Ray at a table by the windows. Ray saw Clyde in almost the same instant and waved him over. "Just in time. You can help me eat this other trout. Caught him myself this morning. Caught two, matter of fact, and the blasted chef cooked 'em both."

"Thanks, but I ate earlier," said Clyde. "I only had a sandwich and coffee on the way down, and I was hungry when I got here."

"Better try one. Nice eating size . . . 'bout a pound and a half apiece. Chef grills 'em with butter and lemon, and I hate to see 'em go to waste."

"They won't if I know you, butterball."

"Sit and starve, then, and see if I care." Roy wasn't precisely a butterball, but he was plump and balding. He was also a top-notch photographer. He chewed a bite of the grilled trout with relish and said somewhat indistinctly: "How do you rate a gravy assignment like this, boy? I thought you were going on vacation."

"You tell me," said Clyde briefly. "Anything cooking on this thing, Ray?"

"Same thing. The killer has evaporated in thin air. About once a day somebody reports they've seen him, and it's always fifty miles from where the last one saw him. The state cops are wearing out the roads, but every report has checked out vacant. When I phoned in to the paper today, they told me you were coming down, so I went out to shoot some pics of the killer's family, and, brother, if you go out for an interview, you take a bodyguard. That there is a bunch of characters, mister."

"I was hoping you'd have some preliminary dope on them

for me. What's the scoop?"

Ray chewed and swallowed. "Look, Clyde, they're right out of Tobacco Road, with a slight overlap of the Hatfields and the McCoys. They don't like nobody. They wouldn't stand still for pictures, so I sneaked a few candids with the thirty-five millimeter, and I got the impression that any one of them above the age of five would have been delighted to bash me over the head and leave me to rot behind the nearest stump. I was just most awful happy that I'd gone with a state trooper. If you get any printable quotes out of them, I'm going to put you in for the hand-tooled leather medal."

"I've got a trunkful of them," said Clyde.

"That's what I like about you, boy . . . your shy, retiring, modest nature." Ray applied himself to the trout for several moments, and then said without looking up: "Saw Kathy today."

That took a moment to sink in. Then Clyde said, easily he hoped: "That so? Where?"

Ray took his time drinking coffee. "Here."

"What do you mean, here?" Despite himself, he sent a quick look around the dining room.

"Here at the lake, where else? I went over to my car for some stuff, and she came out of the store, and we almost bumped into each other, so I said hello, and she said hello, how are you, and I said fine, and she went on down to the dock." He looked at Clyde now, a careful, considering look.

Clyde didn't say anything.

"She looked good," said Ray. "But then, she always did."

Clyde grunted and ran a thumbnail across the tablecloth.

Ray took another swallow of coffee. "Look," he said. "You're both nice people. You're too darned nice people to have this happen. Why don't you get together and try to straighten . . . ?"

126

"Why don't you mind your own damned business?" said Clyde evenly.

Ray sat in silence for a long moment. Then he grunted—"Sure."—threw down his napkin, and got up. He made a one-handed grab at the leather kit bag by his chair, and Clyde said: "I'm sorry, Ray. It's just too . . . I had no right to say that. I apologize."

Ray dug a hand in his pocket and studied the handful of change. "Sure," he said. He dropped a coin on the table and walked over to the cashier's counter and signed his check. Clyde followed him.

"Ray . . . ?" he said.

"Forget it, forget it. None of my business. No right to open my mouth. Now, I really got to go up and see if I remembered to take off the lens cap before I shot this stuff. I'll see you."

Clyde looked around the lobby of the lodge with mixed dread and hope. Then he snorted to himself and went over to the recreation room. Kathy wouldn't likely be here in the lodge, at least. Or would she? He'd heard through mutual friends that she was working in Midland. Midland people came up to the lake to fish and vacation. He shrugged that one off, found himself watching the bingo game, and finally sat in. He won a carton of cigarettes at only three times what it would have cost him over the counter, and went upstairs.

He had Ray's room number, and, when he tapped on the door, Ray immediately squalled that the first thus and such to open the door and let in light would get his skull caved in. Clyde identified himself and got a blistering reply about people who bothered people when people were trying to develop film, and they then made a date through the closed door for fishing at four o'clock the next morning. Clyde went to bed and tossed restlessly and would have sworn that he hadn't slept a wink except that it took him three minutes to find the shrilly shrieking little travel alarm clock he'd set the night before. It was still blacker than inside a cow. And the temperature was decidedly shivery.

He put on fishing clothing and met Ray in the hall, similarly attired. An early-rising waitress in the dining room had coffee made, and both decided to get by on that after they were informed that breakfast would not be available for another hour.

They trolled the shallows of the lower lake until the sun had well-gilded Cowhorn Peak, and then shifted to trolling in the deeps of the upper arm. Clyde got two firm strikes, but failed to hook, and Ray caught a two-pounder and gloated about it all the way back to the dock.

While Ray was in the fish house scaling and cleaning his catch, Clyde saw the State Patrol car and walked over. It was the same Sergeant John Lawe.

Clyde said: "I'm supposed to interview the Tollifer family, Sergeant. Think I'll have any trouble finding them?"

"When do you want to go?"

"Oh, after breakfast. I was just about to eat."

"I'll take you, if you want. You could get crossed up on some of those dirt roads."

"That's too much trouble. Just tell me how to. . . ."

"No trouble. Come by when you're ready."

"Well . . . thanks. Have breakfast with us?"

"Had mine, thanks."

Clyde looked in at the fish house. Ray was lovingly weighing his fish for the third time. "Oh, wash your filthy paws," Clyde told him, "and let's go eat."

"Jealousy, jealousy," murmured Ray.

An inboard cruiser purred quietly and expensively in to the dock, and a slim girl in shorts and a bright blouse stepped out and secured a line. She turned and came toward him, and Clyde suddenly felt his heart give a great wrenching double thump, and an almost panicky dryness came in his throat. He half turned to enter the door beside him, and realized that she was too close to miss that abrupt movement. His fingers went automatically to his shirt pocket and extracted a cigarette, and his other hand brought up his lighter, and he cupped his hands and ducked his head and made an involved business of shielding the flame and lighting the cigarette. Then, finally, it couldn't be postponed any longer, and he looked up.

She had spotted him. She was at the corner of the building, where it abutted the dock, and she was standing stock still and staring at him.

"Hello, Kathy," he said, and his voice sounded flat and faint to his own ears.

"Clyde," she said, almost bewilderedly, almost unbelievingly.

He swallowed the sudden lump in his throat and heard his own queer voice saying intensely: "How are you, Kathy?"

She answered—"Fine."—automatically, and over her shoulder he saw a tall and rangy man rear up from where he had been doing something in the cockpit of the cruiser, and then the tall figure vaulted lightly to the dock and strode toward them. Clyde recognized him. Larry Seaforth. He saw Larry break stride, and then hurry forward, and he dimly heard Kathy say: "But, Clyde, what . . . ?"

"Down on an assignment," he said. He reached up and took a puff on his cigarette. He watched Larry Seaforth take his last two strides and come up behind Kathy, and put a hand on her arm, almost protectively. Larry wore a half smile, but his eyes were watchful. "How are you, Cameron?" he said to Clyde in his level, forceful voice. His tone implied that he didn't give a damn, but that Clyde should.

"Fine," said Clyde, as automatically as Kathy had replied to him.

"Good," said Larry, and his tone said it wasn't at all, and his big, tanned hand on Kathy's arm urged her around and past Clyde.

At Clyde's shoulder, Ray stuck his head out the door and said: "Clyde . . . oh!" He disappeared back inside.

Larry looked around at the sound, gave Clyde a taut half smile, and went on, his hand still on Kathy's arm. Clyde felt a sudden burning pain and shook his hand and swore under his breath. He had clenched his fist on his own burning cigarette, then stepped on the smoldering mass of burning tobacco and paper.

Ray's carefully neutral voice said from beside him: "You ready to go now, Clyde?"

"I guess." He saw Larry almost stoop from his lean height to say something to Kathy, who looked tiny and fragile and utterly desirable, overshadowed as she was by his size, and the burned hand hurt Clyde again as his fingers clenched. He tore his eyes away from them with an effort, and his thoughts said: *Damn, damn, damn, won't I ever get over this?*

He walked with Ray in silence halfway to the lodge, and then Ray murmured: "Shouldn't I know the tall cookie?"

"Larry Seaforth," said Clyde jerkily. "Big-shot family. Seaforth Orchards, Incorporated. Big operators in the valley around Midland. Summer home up here, across the lake. Suppose the old man invited Kathy up for her vacation."

"Yeah, yeah, sure. Old man's a big wheel up at the capital. Farmer's and fruit grower's lobby. Why, he. . . ."

"Yeah?"

"Nothing. I was thinking of something else."

Clyde had a good ear. He'd had enough stories, straight and otherwise, poured into them to know a false note when he heard it. Ray's voice didn't ring. "All right. What is it?"

"It's none of my business. Forget it."

Clyde stopped, and simply looked at him.

"All right, then," said Ray. "My big mouth. The old man isn't here, Clyde. He's up at the capital. He and his wife. I stopped there to shoot some stuff on the legislature on the way. . . ."

Clyde started walking automatically. He didn't hear the last of Ray's words, or even notice the plump little photographer almost trotting to keep up with his own long strides. There wasn't anything in his thoughts that could be translated into words. Just a great, wild churning, burning bitterness that made him sick as a dog and strong as a tiger all at once. His mind did not add sums to come to a result, but leaped to the one bitter, final answer and then instantly rejected that answer as impossible and unworthy of consideration. But the rejected answer bounced back, and his viciously coiled thoughts slashed and struck and ripped it to meaningless shreds while the little bits and shreds were in the very process of squirming back together to make themselves a whole again. Finally he heard Ray speaking, not sensible words, just a vaguely worrying and inquiring sound, and he gathered the whole dark, squirming mass and thrust it back into a compartment where there was no light, no thought, and slowly he came back into that phase of thought where he was not a savage ravening with killing desire, but a sane and sensible man named Clyde Cameron with a friend named Ray Courtney and who hadn't had his breakfast yet.

"Me and my big mouth," said Ray miserably.

Clyde didn't even hear that. He made himself not hear it. He ignored it, and Ray's anxious face, and he said in a perfectly normal and casual voice: "What do you say we eat, buster?"

He didn't remember ordering, or eating, but he must have, for they flipped coins, and Ray paid the check, and the check showed two breakfasts. He was even able to stand on the verandah outside the lobby entrance and watch the cruiser, bright with brass and sleek with mahogany, purring throatily and slicing into the angle of a spreading vee of foamy wake across the lake toward the summer homes. He watched until it was just a creeping bug out in the eye-hurting shimmer, and then he turned and walked stolidly down to where Sergeant John Lawe had his official car parked.

Sergeant Lawe took the paved access road out to Route 222 and turned left. Five miles down the highway he turned off onto a dirt road. Clyde didn't feel like making conversation, and the sergeant's only comment was when he waved a hand at the thickly covered slopes that hemmed in the highway. "I still say our boy's in there. Best cover in the world, and him as wild as anything that lives there."

"Suppose a plane would do any good spotting?" asked Clyde.

"Any bush big enough to hide a dog would cover him, and he could hear a plane a mile off."

After that, they rode in silence broken only once by the muttering of the radio speaker.

A few hundred yards into the brush, the dirt road forked, and another black coupé was parked just clear of the fork. A trooper who looked as though he couldn't have been much more than a high-school graduate came strolling around the car with a lever-action carbine hooked on his arm.

"Hi, Sarge."

"Wendell. Anything doing?"

"Quiet. I could use some more coffee."

"You'll live. This is Clyde Cameron, Wendell. Reporter for the *Register*. If you see him running around loose, don't shoot him unless he can't fork up an I D. Trooper Jim Wendell, Clyde."

The boy-faced trooper shifted the carbine to shake hands, and the sergeant put the car in gear. "Check with me when you go by the lake tonight, will you, Wendell?"

"Sure thing, Sarge." The trooper sketched a salute and strolled back to his car.

"Looks young enough," said Clyde as the sergeant's car whined and jounced softly on the dirt road.

"Don't let that fool you," said the sergeant. "He's been in the service five years, and he can take care of himself." He chuckled suddenly. "Every time he stops some woman for a traffic boner, though, he has a bad time. The older ones give him a motherly talking to, and the younger ones think he's cute. They really give him a bad time."

The radio speaker snarled out a code phrase, and the sergeant stiffened, sent a searching look ahead, dropped the shift lever to low, and made a dirt-scattering U-turn in a space that Clyde would have sworn was far too small for the maneuver.

The sergeant unhooked his mike, thumbed the button, recited a number, and demanded: "Who was it?"

"Don't know," the speaker blurted out.

"O K. There in two minutes. Out."

The sergeant drove hard at the Y-fork of the roads, stabbed at the brakes, tramped the gas pedal, took the tight turn in a flat slide, bellowing at the boyish trooper as he passed: "Stay here . . . keep awake!" Then he drove the black coupé snarling up this new road that soon resolved into a mere double-wheel track that unconcernedly turned at right angles to avoid trees and on which only the sketchiest effort had been made to remove the larger rocks and holes. Clyde put a bracing hand on the dash and another on the window edge and got it slapped with a clump of pine needles. At least twice he was ready to swear that the car frame had to bend to let them around a turn. It was roughly equivalent to threading a needle while clapping one's hands briskly. They made one last, soaring jounce and a tight left turn, and the sergeant hit the brakes.

A rough pole-and-shake cabin was huddled back in the brush, a hundred feet or so from the truck. A spring bubbled up nearby, with a coffee can upended on a stake beside it. A uniformed patrolman, looking slightly rumpled and in need of a shave, stood by the corner of the cabin, eyeing the sergeant's car watchfully. He carried a rifle, too, in addition to the regulation walnut-butted pistol in the polished holster against his thigh. Sergeant Lawe slammed his car door behind him and stalked toward the patrolman. He said: "O K."

"Well, it looks like somebody got in last night, that's all, Sarge. We were watching it. . . ."

The sergeant snarled violently. "Weren't you supposed to be *in* that damned shack?"

"Well, yeah, but damn it, Sarge, it stinks in there, and you split up, one in and one out, and you can't keep awake, and you can't smoke, and holy cow, Sarge, three nights in a row now, and not so much as a damned porcupine around. . . ."

The sergeant clenched his fists and wheeled away and then back, and his voice cracked: "So you came out and kegged up with your backs to a tree and talked yourselves to sleep."

The trooper flushed. "Well, maybe we did doze off, taking turns. But one of us was awake all the time . . . damn it, Sarge, three nights in a row, and. . . ."

The sergeant still hulked over him, glowering, working his clenched fists. Then he took a deep breath and relaxed. "O K," said Sergeant Lawe tiredly. "What's missing?"

"Well, grub . . . canned stuff and bacon and coffee. And

134

. . . and the ammunition, Sarge."

"What!"

The trooper swallowed convulsively and said: "Yeah. We bundled it up, remember, and hid it under . . . ?"

The sergeant breathed hard through his nose. "O K." He walked toward the shack, and Clyde followed without invitation. They found another trooper with a radio in a leather field case between his knees as he sat on the ground by the corner of the shack. He was listening intently to earphones, and, as they came up, he took up the microphone and murmured something, holding the mike almost against his lips. He snapped a key and shucked off the earphones and looked up at Sergeant Lawe.

"The captain's coming in," he said. "Sorry about the delay, Sarge. Mac hollered at me, and startled me so that I hooked my damned clumsy foot in the shoulder strap of the case here, and kicked it halfway across the flat. Had a helluva time tracing out what jarred loose."

"Yeah, sure," said the sergeant. He walked over to the split board door of the shack and yanked it open. Clyde moved up to look over his shoulder. Dark as a pocket, it did smell. The musty odor of bed clothing long unwashed, old and rancid grease, other things old and unclean. The sergeant produced a flashlight, flicked a pale beam about the shack, revealing a jumbled clutter which didn't look quite normal even for the abode of a man who seemed to prefer living like an animal. He grunted and backed out, almost bumping into Clyde and showing him a wry face.

"Think it was Tollifer?" asked Clyde.

"I'd bet money on it."

"Now what?"

"We wait for the captain." He turned away and walked toward the spring.

Clyde took a small notebook out of his pocket and moved over to the two troopers by the radio.

"Hi," he said. "I heard the sergeant call you Herb. Herb what?"

The trooper looked him over with a cop's impersonal eye. "Who're you?"

"Clyde Cameron. I work on the *Register*."

Without looking away, the trooper raised his voice. "Sarge, this guy O K?"

The sergeant was drinking water at the spring. He nodded and swallowed and said: "O K." He splashed the rest of the water out of the can and hung it back on the stake and tramped down to them. "You can write this and make us look like a pack of awful damned fools," he said.

"We'll see how it goes," said Clyde briefly. He looked inquiringly at Herb, who hesitated and said finally: "Herb Cryder. My partner here's Bert MacLain."

Clyde asked MacLain whether it was Mac or Mc, nodded his thanks, and put the notebook away. He asked the sergeant about this cabin.

Lawe said: "Roy's a loner. He'd hang around his folks a while, and then he'd take off for the high lonesome. Keg up here for months, sometimes, eating venison and grouse and just hunting and trapping. Now he's got grub and ammunition. There went our leverage. He'll kill somebody else now, before we get him."

They heard a car coming, down the rough road. The sergeant said with what sounded to Clyde like resignation: "That will be the captain."

The captain was lean as a whip and straight as a ramrod. He got out of his car with quick precision, closed the door quietly. His uniform fit him like a second skin, boots and belt glittering with a glassy sheen, visored cap set squarely on his neatly made, close-cropped head. He wore his powder-blue uniform as a West Pointer wears his full dress. Clyde made a mental note for his story.

The captain's hawk-look pinned Clyde a moment, studying, inventorying, went back to Sergeant Lawe. "What's the word, John?" His voice was crisp, military.

"He's been here," said John Lawe. "Got himself some grub . . . and some more ammo. It couldn't be helped."

"Why not? Man on guard here, wasn't there?"

"Two. Just stepped outside for a little while. . . ."

"Supposed to be inside, wasn't he?"

The big sergeant said evenly: "Herb's been on it three days. Bert about the same. That dump smells like a gut wagon. I'd have stepped out, too."

"Yes," said the captain. He looked at Clyde. "Who is this young man?"

The sergeant introduced them. "Glad to know you," said the captain, sounding not at all glad, then turned and strode to the cabin. He stood in its sty-like confines, pivoted in a full circle, exploring with a probing flashlight beam, stalked out.

"We'll burn it," he said crisply. "I'll have them send in a pickup with a pump from the smoke-chaser camp. You two stand by with me. You can carry on with whatever you were doing, Sergeant."

"Yes, sir," said Sergeant Lawe. He turned toward his car, Clyde following.

The captain said: "You understand you've other duties besides chauffeuring reporters?"

Said Sergeant John Lawe stiffly, woodenly: "I know my job, Captain."

He got no reply to that, and he started the car, turned it, and undertook the jouncing, thread-needle passage back, not fast this time.

137

Clyde finally broke the rather thick atmosphere with: "Cool character, isn't he?"

"He's all right," said the big sergeant. "The Army made a second lieutenant out of him once, and he never got over it. But he's all right. He's mad, just like the rest of us, but he can't beller and faunch around and get it out of his system, the way I do."

The radio speaker snapped, then emitted the captain's voice, crisp and militarily-toned even through the gargling effect of the short-wave set, requesting a light pumper from the fire protection group camp.

Clyde said tentatively: "You don't have to drive me up to the Tollifers. I can probably find it myself."

"No, it's all right. He was just blowing off. I'm supposed to make a head count every day, anyway."

This road was slightly less primitive and so was the house. It was made of sawed lumber, board-and-battens upright on the outside, and it had been painted at some distant time. There was a ramshackle barn beyond and an assortment of sheds and lean-tos. A covey of red hens scratched and clucked at the side of the house. There was the air and odor of careless poverty, even to the remains of ancient stumps in the fields, so old that they were no more than slumping mounds of punky wood. The weathered porch had a sagging roof and on the step sat a slender young man in Army suntans, *sans* tie and cap. It took a determined soldier to keep suntans looking neat, as Clyde well knew, and this one looked particularly sloppy. He watched the police car approach and managed to express a complete contempt and insolence; perhaps it was no more than his natural expression. As Sergeant Lawe stepped out of the car, the young man ostentatiously stretched a leg, reached into a pocket, brought out a long-bladed jackknife and began peeling paper-thin shavings from a stick.

"Hello, cop," he said. It was a dirty word, the way he said it.

"Hello, soldier," said Sergeant Lawe. It was a disgusted word, the way he said it.

The young man grinned—as a wolf grins—showing sharp, yellowed teeth. "You don't like my soldier suit, cop? Too bad. I didn't ask f'r't, though. They come an' got me, an' give it to me."

"So I hear. Dragged you out from under the bed, didn't they?"

The grin stretched, malicious and unhumorous. "Naw, they never. And it only took four of them soldier cops to whip me. 'Course, I only had my bare naked hands. Who's this dude with you . . . gover'ment cop? Roy really gettin' you boys to stirrin' 'round?"

"No," said Sergeant John Lawe. "If he was a federal man, I expect we'd have to go in and drag Roy out from under the bed."

The soldier's lips puckered, and he spat. "Fuck you! If you thought Roy's 'thin five mile of here, ain't no six o' you cops'd have the guts to drive up to this dooryard . . . with a machine gun cocked and loaded and a six-shooter in each boot!"

"Oh, he's a tough one," agreed the sergeant broadly. "From behind . . . in the dark. No, this man's a reporter . . . from a paper up north. Says he wants to talk to you people. Clyde, this is Roy Tollifer's younger brother, Lafe. Lafe, Clyde Cameron."

Ignoring this last, the man said jeeringly: "From in front, cop . . . in broad daylight . . . 'f I hollered . . . 'Hey, Roy' . . . right now, you'd hunt a hole to crawl in." His eyes flicked at

Clyde, and with scarcely a change of breath or tone he said: "Gonna write about Roy, 'ey? Why the hell don't you write the truth, then?"

Clyde said mildly. "All you've got to do is tell me the truth. I'll write it, Lafe. Now, you're in the Army, I take it . . . any other brothers and sisters, besides Roy?"

"Oh, I'm *in*, mister. Servin' my time. You see, you don't have to *do* nothin' to get in the Army. Man's got rights, they tell me. They can't put you in no jail 'less they got somethin' you done wrong. But you don't have to do nothin' with the Army, mister . . . they want you, they just come an' *git* you. An' you're *in*, mister . . . an' I don't see no hell of a lot of difference from bein' in jail."

Clyde, deciding to go along with it, said easily: "I put in a hitch, too, Lafe. Wasn't too bad, when you didn't have anyone shooting at you."

"Hell, I ain't afraid of no shootin'. Ner Roy, either. You know he got about ever' medal there is, and then they threw him out with a dishonorable discharge? I'd like to've seen their face when he told them pus-gut officers what they could do with it!"

"That so?" said Clyde. "Now that might be something for a story. Got any of them around . . . the medals?"

He got a quick, sidelong flick of the eyes. "He give 'em away . . . threw 'em away. He didn't want nothin' that was no part of the god-damn' Army. I don't blame 'im."

"It strikes some people that way," said Clyde. "How about your brother? Think he'll come in voluntarily when he's had a chance to think it over?"

Lafe cut a malicious look at Lawe. "Hell, he's got nothin' to come in for. Stumble-footed cop falls down an' likely shoots hisself with his own gun, an' the rest of these cops want to hang Roy for it. Naw, he ain't goin' to come in . . . an'

140

those cops ain't likely to go after him, neither. You can write that in your paper. Any time these cops can't find nothin' else to do, they come around an' try to hang somethin' on Roy or me."

Clyde decided he wasn't going to get much out of this one. He asked again: "How many others in your family? Brothers? Sisters?"

"Ask your cop friend. He's got us all down in his little black book."

"How about your mother? Suppose I could speak to her?"

"No, you ain't goin' to speak to her. If she wanted to talk to you, she'd come out an' talk to you, but she don't, and this is private property, an' you ain't pushin' nobody around here."

Clyde shrugged and looked at John Lawe.

The sergeant said crisply: "Let's see your leave papers, soldier."

Lafe gave the sergeant a long scrutiny. Then his face twisted in bitterness, and he slowly reached into a hip pocket. "Makes you happy to watch 'em squirm, don't it, cop? All right, here's your damn' papers. You know what you can do with 'em."

"Take 'em out of the billfold," said Sergeant Lawe, impersonally official. "I just want the papers."

He was handed the crumpled sheet. He read it carefully, refolded it, said: "You've got two days, and it's five hundred miles back to camp. When are you leaving?"

"When I get damn' good and ready."

"You'd better get ready."

"I get some grace time."

"Not with me, you don't. This is for your own good, Lafe. Smarten up. Roy filled you full of stuff about the Army, and you're headed the same way he went. Wise up, boy. Buck up

141

that uniform and go along with the book. You can come out of there a better man than when you went in. Or you can make the stockade inside and the jail outside."

"You bet, cop. An' you'll be just the thus and such that'll do it, too, ain't you?"

"That could be. You get what you wanted, Clyde?"

"Looks like I've got all I'm going to get," said Clyde. "I'm ready when you are."

"O K. And Lafe . . . you can tell Roy, if you see him, that he won't be squatting in that shack any more. The captain just had it burned down."

Lafe shot a quick, incredulous look at the trooper. "You burned Roy's cabin?"

"It wasn't his . . . that's state land, you know, and he didn't build it. He can come in and claim his stuff, if he wants it."

Lafe's eyes were brilliant with emotion. "You burned Roy's cabin! You'll sweat for that one, cop. Oh, you'll be a sorry bunch of bastards for that one!"

"There's a complaint department down at the barracks," said the sergeant dryly. "Send him down."

In the car again, Clyde jotted notes and asked: "How about this medal business, Sergeant?"

"You mean Roy? No, he never got any medals. We've got his service record. He got his theater ribbons and made Expert Rifleman, but outside of that he didn't even get a Good Conduct ribbon. He drew enough company punishment to last a man through a hundred-year hitch, but he missed the stockade. They finally shook him loose with a dishonorable. Oh, he's a nice guy. Y'know, they get up these summer camps . . . get the kids out of the slums and into the clean air . . . does wonders for some of 'em. Here's Roy . . . never lived in a town of more than fifty people in his life, lives like a pig in the prettiest outdoors in the world, got all the instincts of a half-tame bear coming in to rob the garbage pits. Maybe you could tell me why?"

"Not me," said Clyde. "I'm no head shrinker. I just call 'em as they fall, and then they hash it up in rewrite."

"Ought to try it as a cop some time. But then, I guess neither one of us was drafted into it. This could be a break, in one way, though. The captain can get more men, maybe, now that we know he's still here and loaded with ammunition."

"Can I quote you on that?"

"No, because the captain's in charge. And I doubt he'll release anything till he's ready to move. But that's your business."

"So it is. If you'll drop me off at the resort, I'll phone in what I've got."

"Like I say," said Sergeant John Lawe, "you can write it to make us look like a bunch of damned fools."

Clyde grinned thinly. "You can read all about it in the paper," he said.

"Sure," said Sergeant Lawe. He didn't sound hopeful.

Clyde phoned in a factual, straightaway story on the new developments. When he had finished dictating, Bill Dawson came on the wire and ripped into him savagely. "What's your follow-up, Clyde? Damn it, not one word to the effect that the manhunt is being intensified . . . no dragnet stuff . . . no statement from the quote . . . grim-faced Captain Mudface who said . . . unquote. Crying in a bucket, Clyde? You want me to send you a mimeo cub sheet to check off questions and answers on? Now listen . . . get on that captain's back and don't get off till we get the quotes and answers. Make like a reporter, man."

"Listen to yourself, buster," said Clyde. "I can't get on his back. All he's got to do is take off down the road at eighty miles an hour on 'official business,' and, when I follow, he has a trooper pick me off and cite me for reckless driving, or whatever. You go ahead and whipsaw him in print, and he won't even give me the time of day. These aren't city cops, Bill. Each car and trooper is pretty near an independent unit. Put somebody on it at State Headquarters . . . the public relations man there will be more susceptible to the pressure you can put on. And don't try to tell me how to do my job. Anytime you ain't happy, buster, just get yourself another boy. Matter of fact, that's a helluva good idea. Write out my severance pay and send it down here. I quit."

"In a pig's eye, you quit! You run out on an assignment, and the only thing you'll work at for the next five years will be reporting farm news for some hick weekly in a town of three hundred population, period. You just soothe your aching tail feathers and get on it. What's the situation . . . you getting no co-operation from the gendarmes?"

"They're playing it close to the vest." He'd made his point, with his threat to quit, and did not need to twist the knife. "I've got one fair contact, and I can cultivate more. I'll get whatever is available as fast as anyone else, and, if that isn't satisfactory, I refer you back to our previous conversation, and good night to you, Billy boy."

"Just a minute, Clyde. I want that first feature in the mail by tomorrow. Is Ray getting any pics?"

"Said he got some. I'll work on it tonight."

"O K. Good bye. And get with it, will you, Clyde?"

He hung up without answering that query, stepped out of the phone booth into the lobby, and looked absently through the view windows across the sparkling lake. Idly he wondered where Ray Courtney might be, and idly he considered the idea of a little evening fishing. Almost as idly, he knew he had no real inclination for it, and felt a touch of wonder at that. He knew the why of his disinterest, and almost forcibly crammed it back out of thought. There wasn't much he could do on the killer story but wait, and he could remember the time when waiting drove him nearly batty, and right now he just didn't give a damn. Dimly he knew this disinterest was dangerous to him, in a subtle and gnawing way, and he dropped into a rustically styled but comfortable chair, lighted a cigarette, and stared broodingly across the lovely, sparkling expanse of the lake and slowly gave himself to thoughts of his personal problem. It was not particularly pleasant, and he did not enjoy it. In one sense, he must wait. In another he could not wait. Once committed to that, he had a beginning. Maybe one day he'd have an answer. Finally he let out a short, gusty sigh, and went upstairs. He had a story to write.

In this primitive forest, in parts almost untouched since creation perhaps, were trees that were old when a dreamer named Columbus set out in his little cockleshells to find a new world. Here were ripe, old giants that had been flourishing saplings when they nailed Him to a cross of still more ancient timbers at the place called Golgotha. Here were trees that stubbornly resisted snow's crushing weight while Napoléon shivered in his retreat on faraway steppes, had felt the weight of a thousand such winters when barefoot men stood sentry duty in Valley Forge. All unheeding, they had stood, these millennia, knowing nothing save the built-in urge of survival that thrust them in growth toward an unattainable sky, to reach their limit of growth, simply to endure, to ripen, to one day die. They stood unheeding now of the man who moved among them, as a wary blacktail deer would move, in a slow pacing and a pausing and a listening waiting—to go on again in that slow, alert, and watchful way.

The hunted ones move this way, those who survive their first hunt. So, too, do the wise hunters move, for the blundering quarry does not survive—the blundering hunter will starve, or otherwise die in his turn. His eyes showed a dullness, this preoccupied man, the dullness of one whose thoughts turn inward. He moved as of long habit, and his harking alertness was that of a natural inborn thing, carried out without conscious thought.

His scant clothing was threadbare, almost completely worn out evenly all over. His beard was a scraggly growth of pitch blackness, the growth of a week or more, not yet long enough to be changed from bristly scrub to softer hair. His skin was dark, weather-dark and dirty-dark, his face above the shirt, his elbow where it showed through a burst-through sleeve, his hands, which held a rifle. The rifle was the cleanest thing about him, although the walnut stock was nicked and marked with hard use, the barrel and magazine tube beneath and the lever action all showing the highlights of rubbing and wear. It was carried as casually and thoughtlessly as a stick, but in that very casualness was the assurance of complete familiarity. So casually does a wild bull carry his goring horns, a wolf his glinting saber teeth, a rattlesnake his daggered fangs—casually, thoughtlessly, competently.

The man harked long, alertly, motionlessly, in a little glade shadowed and cool, fenced around by great, towering, shaggy-barked trees. There was a tinkling, watery sound and the unalarmed chirping of birds. Once the scuttling sound of some small forest dweller cautiously speeding from shelter to shelter. From complete stillness the man relaxed to quiet movement, stepped easily forward, and knelt to drink where bubbling water forced its way with liquid insistence between mossy rocks and then softly tinkled free in a little run of only a few yards before again sinking into the receptive earth. The wild ones knew this place, for their marks were all about.

The man had his drink, then unslung a slackly loaded, dirty sack from his shoulder, scrabbled through it, and brought out a can, flat on top and bottom, oval in perimeter's shape. He unsnapped a heavy wire key from its attachment, wound crisply tearing tinplate on it, opening the top, shoveled out sardines coated with mustard sauce with his fingers, fed on them directly from the can as fast as he could lift and chew and swallow. At the end, he tipped the can and drank oil and sauce, and then carelessly threw the can aside and again rooted in the bag.

He came up with a can of corned beef, in a tapered pedestal shape, again opened and ate gulpingly, hungrily, wolfishly. Later he sat slackly, looking broodingly across the little spring and its seep, into the palisade of thick-boled timber beyond.

It was not an old face; it might have been called an almost handsome face, had it been cleaned and barbered and firmed with purposefulness. Now it was like still water, not placid, but unstirring, save when some unguessable thought brought small changes of expression, stirring the surface like the movement of some unseen creature just beneath it. He looked at the discarded food tins, unstirring, broodingly, finally moved to where they had been carelessly tossed, retrieved them, took them over beyond the encircling trees, thrust them under a covering of the carpet of forest duff, brushing absently at the scuffed place to better assure their concealment.

He blinked slowly, sleepily, moved at his slow, harking gait a hundred feet or so, and retreated into deeper brush, backing himself into a thick clump, lay with his lop-brimmed hat as cushion between his head and grub sack, his rifle under his hand, commanding the way he had come. He shrugged and squirmed his hips and shoulders to casual comfort as a dog might, breathed a short gusty sigh, and almost instantly dozed off. Around him the soft sounds went on, as undisturbed as if he had never been. Like any hunted animal, the killer was secure for the moment, fed and replenishing his strength, asleep to restore his alertness, waiting, with unthinking patience, for his good chance to come.

Clyde Cameron uncased his portable typewriter in his room, set it up on a low table with paper and carbons cranked in, spread his morgue clips in the sequence he wanted, finally typed in caps—**MANHUNT!**—his byline below, spaced down, indented, and began:

At beautiful Sapphire Lake, carefree vacationers are playing—fishing, swimming, boating, sunning themselves. Children are scampering on sandy beaches, splashing and shrieking in cool, clear water. Almost within sound of their happy shouting, grim-faced, determined men are hunting another man. They move carefully, these men, speaking quietly or not at all, watching alertly—for this is the most deadly of all hunts, and a killer is at large, a killer without compunction—a killer who now has nothing to lose. . . .

Clyde frowningly read it over, grimaced slightly, decided to let it stand. This wasn't a news story, but a feature, frosting on the cake, and a little melodrama was permissible. He lighted a cigarette, again scanned the clips, and settled down to writing the story. It went well, paged until it had his required wordage. He read it through, carefully checked his direct quotes and assured himself of his "alleged" and "suspected" labels wherever he used Roy Tollifer's name directly. He snapped out his carbons and flimsies, again checked his penciled corrections, and then folded the originals, addressed and stamped the envelope, took it down to the lobby, and put it in the outgoing mail, then wandered restlessly around the lobby. They were showing a movie in the recreation room, a colored picture of boatmen running the rapids on Rogue River in Oregon. They had a good crowd, and above the booming of the narrator's voice he could hear their gasps of delighted, vicarious fright as the boats soared and fell and splashed wetly into near disaster, and somehow he was in no mood for such entertainment.

He went into the almost deserted dining room and ordered coffee, sat sipping it absently, and considering what means he could use to get next to Captain Carrington. With word out now that the killer was definitely within the triangle, resupplied with food and ammunition, it was almost a cinch the opposition papers would send reporters down on the story, and in simple loyalty to his job Clyde wanted anything as near to an inside track as he could get. But it would be a little like snuggling up to a porcupine to get next to the good captain.

He saw through the dining room doorway when Ray Courtney came across the lobby, and beckoned him in. Ray had an envelope labeled **PHOTOGRAPHS—DO NOT FOLD** in his hand. He dropped in on the table, said—"Coffee, honey."— to the waitress, and to Clyde: "Getting anything done?"

"Not much," said Clyde. "You?"

Ray shrugged. "Shot a little cheesecake out on the lake this afternoon, worked up some prints. You get to see the Tollifer tribe? I got some extra prints here."

"You missed the fire, then," said Clyde.

"What fire?"

Clyde told him about the burning of Roy Tollifer's shack.

Ray swore. "My buddy," he said bitterly. "My faithful chum."

"Get you a big ol' bird dog," suggested Clyde. "Have somebody train him, so you can follow him around while he points out pictures for you. Besides, if I had whistled, you wouldn't have heard it, ten miles away."

"Oh, hush," said Ray, "you make me sick. Here . . . no, by golly, I got half a mind to make you go look at those Tollifers yourself. Just like you helped me." But he slid the glossy prints across to Clyde.

Mrs. Tollifer, mother of Roy and Lafe, was a woman of indeterminate years, as shapeless in her sagging cotton dress as a meal sack loosely cinched with string; her face was as malleable and characteristic as putty, at least in Ray Courtney's picture, and the putty had sagged, before setting, into an expression of dull apprehension. There were shots of a couple of girls, just short of their teens, in need of washing and combing, a boy of six or seven, *ditto,* who stood staring at the viewer with an expression that could have been snarling or just the result of squinting into the sun. Lafe's picture was blurred, as if he had charged the camera at first sight of it, which Ray said he had. "Took a swing at me," he said, "but I ducked behind a big cop."

"My hero," said Clyde.

"All I had to defend myself with," said Ray, "was my light meter. I should bust that on his worthless skull?"

"Not when there's a big cop handy," agreed Clyde. He shuffled through the rest of the photos, glanced at one with a sudden lurching feeling inside, stopped, stared at it longer. Ray caught that, hunched forward, and looked, too.

"Didn't mean to put that one in," he said.

It was Kathy, and Ray had caught a good picture, even in this small, glossy print. He had caught her in profile, on the dock, nicely backlighted against the lake. Abstractly it was lovely, and deeply, personally, intimately Clyde knew just how lovely. It was a pretty girl's face, but to Clyde Cameron it was Kathy's face, and he knew it in all angles and all lights, every line, every curve, every shade of coloring. The picture showed a pretty girl's figure, in blouse and white shorts; she could wear shorts, and she had beautifully shaped legs; Clyde knew her every beauty and every blemish, head to toe, and the blemishes were precious few; he felt the glossy-faced square of thick paper trembling in his fingers—carefully he kept expression of his feelings off his face. He hid that picture until the last in the same shuffling movement he had given the rest, went through more pictures of pretty girls—girls on water skis, on diving floats, girls laughing archly, preening themselves in tight bathing suits for the camera—just pretty girls' pictures, meaningless in themselves, all save one, and that one meaningful only to Clyde Cameron, who felt like a fool, a clumsily drowning fool, full of a dull regret and a silly yearning that was as simple as it was unexplainable, even to himself. Because she was his wife, and she was not—she was a strange and pretty girl in a photograph, and as much a part of him as his own hands. And carefully he said nothing, showed nothing, going through the pictures, squaring them into a compact deck with his finger tips, handing them back to Ray Courtney. Ray looked relieved.

He said apologetically: "Profiled and backlighted like that, by the time the engravers get done with it, it won't be anything but a nice mild cheesecake. I won't even send it in to use, if you say so."

"Why the hell is it my say so?" demanded Clyde roughly. "If you were going to make a big production out of it, why didn't you hide it in your wallet? Why do you keep beating me over the head with it?"

"Ah, hell," said Ray, discomfited. He was a butterball, and a nice guy, and an old news-lens man. His camera had peeked coyly at pretty girls, caught faces laughing and tragic, clicked dismally over dead ones sprawling gracelessly in the aftermath of violence; his quick roundness was case-hardened and glass-sharp at the edges; he was seldom shocked or surprised or dismayed, yet inside he was as sentimental as a fond grandmother—and would have fought the man with his fists who said so. He gave Clyde a hangdog look now but pursued bravely: "Sure, it's none of my business, but I hate to see it happen. It hadn't ought to happen. I know a hundred damn' fools I wouldn't give a snap of my fingers about, and another hundred where a split-up would be better all around . . . but not you two. Damn it, I'm your friend, Clyde . . . to both of you. I wish there was something I could do."

"You show me anything anybody outside can do," said Clyde flatly, "and I'll buy it. Damn it, Ray, who are you trying out for, Miss Lonelyhearts? The thing was inside, with us . . . I didn't find the answers, and I was in it. Sure, all you got to say is . . . 'Grow up, kids, both of you . . . think it out.' . . . and, when you're all through, it's right back to two people having to decide whether they'd rather be miserable together or miserable apart. No, that's speaking for myself. I don't know how it is with her . . . apart. I don't know anything about her any more. But she wanted out, and she got out, and that's the end of it. So who said it was easy? It wasn't easy when Uncle Sam called me back for Korea. It wasn't easy when she lost the baby. It wasn't easy one little bit anywhere along the way . . . and I'd sure as hell appreciate it if you'd let it alone! I don't know how to make it any plainer than that, Ray."

Clyde got out, feeling shaken and taut all in one, feeling ashamed at the expression he'd brought to Ray's face, feeling half angry and half confused, and with the certain knowledge clear and unconfused of his own misery and knowing there wasn't one damned thing to do but learn to live with it. He dropped a quarter on the table and went out, leaving Ray still seated. And because he didn't know where else to go, he went up to his room, closed the door behind him as if to cut off all the world outside, found a chair without turning on a light, and sat, looking across the lake, bemused and only half seeing the lights and their reflection at the dock below, the distant star-winking of light and reflection from the summer homes across the lake under the loom of encircling timbered mountains and the encompassing darkness from the only faintly paler night sky.

Kathy was over there, right now. He pushed that thought aside. With Larry Seaforth. He clubbed that on aside.

For at least an hour he sat, smoking, staring broodingly, not seeing, not thinking, really, finally stirred himself, squinting when he turned on the lights, feeling a sudden violent headache coming on. He took two aspirins and went to bed. In the darkness his head thudded dully. He did not sleep well.

Clyde went down to breakfast early, ate in the company of early fishermen, afterward went down to the dock, where a State Patrol car was parked just at the end of the boathouse. This morning it was the boyish-faced one, Jim Wendell.

He greeted the trooper, was recognized, given an open-faced grin. "Up early," said Wendell.

"Both of us," said Clyde. "Anything cooking?"

"We're getting some help, I understand. Maybe we can corner him this time."

"How much help?"

He got a quick, evaluating look almost completely concealed by the ingenuous smile. "Don't know exactly."

"Who'll be in danger?"

"Why, the captain, I suppose. And then there's Sergeant Lawe and another sergeant along with what troopers they send."

"Where would I find Sergeant Lawe?"

"He's off duty. 'Bout time. I don't think he's slept four nights in the last week and a half."

"How about the captain . . . where'd I find him?"

"He's on the road, somewhere. Patrolling, setting up his line. . . ."

Clyde said deliberately: "What does a man have to do to get information out of you birds? What do you think this is . . . a big spy hunt in Casablanca? If it is, where the hell are all the gorgeous women?"

The ingenuous boyish smile faded slightly. "Don't ask me," the trooper said finally. "I'm just a buck private in the rear rank. I don't know nothing about nothing, nohow."

Clyde said bitterly: "You boys want kid glove treatment from the papers, and then give us the run-around, is that it? Well, maybe you think this is a private war, but the public wants to know what's going on, too, and it's my job to get the story. So you can't catch your man and you're making like a bunch of cloak and dagger artists, and I'm supposed to sit around and play patty cake. Nobody knows anything. Sure. But let you catch somebody, and you'll be shouldering to get in the picture. Then we'll have a dozen stories that . . . confidentially . . . every one of you was the one who *really* cracked it. And you'll be screaming like turpentined tomcats, if I misspell a name or leave out a middle initial. You think, if we don't get anything out of you, we can't write about it. Well, the hell we can't, buster! Now if you want me to walk around and write what I see and guess at what the cops are doing, fine. I'm a damned good guesser. Or you can let me in on it, so I can see what's going on, and get a break in the stories, if you've got one coming. And if the captain isn't too damned busy, I'd certainly appreciate a chance to talk to him."

The boy-faced trooper said with just a touch of steel in his soft voice: "Don't try to threaten me, mister."

"It's no threat. It's a statement of policy. I seem to have bumped into yours. Now you know mine. I don't go around threatening people. You just play it the way you see it."

Clyde got a close and level regard of long moment. Then the trooper murmured finally: "I'll check in. Maybe he'll talk to you and maybe he won't."

"If you'll tell me where," said Clyde patiently, "I'll find him. I'm not trying to foul up his job."

"Sure," said the trooper. He went to his car and unshipped his microphone. In response to a code phrase, the speaker scratched and crackled with another code phrase.

The trooper cleared his throat. "The . . . uh . . . reporter, Mister Cameron, wants to see you, Captain. Should I send him out?"

Even on the crackly speaker, the captain's military tone came through. "You may inform the reporter that all developments are being forwarded through State Headquarters, and that they are issuing news releases and bulletins whenever there is anything to release. May I respectfully recommend he go to that qualified source."

The trooper grinned faintly at Clyde. "You heard him," he said.

Clyde told the trooper succinctly and pointedly what the captain could do with the news releases from State Headquarters, got a thinner grin, and an edited and expurgated transmission of that to the captain.

There was a long pause, while the speaker hummed monotonously, and then the crisp comment: "I will be at the resort sometime after noon. He may see me then, but he is not to regard it as a press conference. You will further observe air silence until you have something of importance to report."

The trooper reddened, spoke an acknowledging code phrase clearly and precisely, and hung up. "Best I can do for you," he said.

"Thanks," said Clyde. "And if I sounded a little uppity, I'm sorry. I've got a job to do, too, you know."

"Sure," said the trooper.

"How about Sergeant Lawe? Where might he be? But you said he was off-duty."

"Yeah. He's been shacking up here at the resort, though. Ought to be pulling in any time. You might catch him."

"O K." He talked to the trooper a while longer, got a look at the operational map they were using, with squares marked and numbered for quick reference in coded instructions. It looked big and complicated, even on a map. Clyde thanked him, jotted a few notes, and went to find his own car.

Where the resort access road met the highway, a trooper he didn't know stopped him and checked his credentials.

"Cameron," he said, and grinned faintly. "Where have I heard that name before?"

Clyde glanced at the black State Patrol car with its motor running and the radio volume turned up. "On the air, maybe," he said dryly.

"Could be," said the trooper. "Where you going?"

"Up the highway . . . why?"

"Don't pick up any hitchhikers. If you see a brush rat with a rifle, you run like hell, and stop the first state car you see."

"Sure," said Clyde.

He cruised the highway at moderate speed, watching the dusty mouths of dirt side roads for signs of traffic. He took an easy, sweeping curve, came quite suddenly on a familiar black car parked on the highway shoulder, saw almost in the same moment the blue-clad figure prone by a rear wheel, had a suddenly frightening knowledge of danger, and then the figure rolled on its side, beckoned urgently at him with a wide-sweeping arm. He hit the brakes, drew abreast the State Patrol car, and hit the brakes again as Sergeant Lawe reared up, gave him one sweeping, recognizing glance, and threw a rifle and a riot gun into back seat of Clyde's car, and swung into the seat alongside Clyde all in one continuing motion. "Get out of here quick," he said. It wasn't loud, or even particularly urgently spoken, but it sent a shiver up Clyde's spine, and he dropped the lever to low and burned rubber taking off. Lawe was looking back, past his own abandoned car. As they continued the sweep of the curve and it fell from sight, he hitched around on the seat, staring ahead, leaning forward, said through his teeth: "Roll this heap, mister! Every second counts, now. Oh, man, am I glad to see you!"

Clyde touched sixty in seconds, dropped into high. The convertible squatted and settled to its work. "What happened?" said Clyde above the wind roar.

"Our boy's back there. Set a trap for me, and I pretty near got suckered. Missed me, but shot up my car. Couldn't move it, couldn't even radio. *Move* this thing!"

The needle was touching 85 as they hit the straightway. Clyde went to 90 . . . 92 . . . 94. He didn't even flick his eyes down to check after that. The wind was a constant, roaring, ear-buffetting pressure. Far ahead he saw a blinding ball of light-glint, reflection from an approaching windshield. Sergeant Lawe leaned close, shouted above the roar: "Pull down! We . . . stop 'em!"

Clyde nodded, lifted his foot a trifle, fearful of what would happen to the tightly wound-up motor if he slacked off too fast, lifted his left foot, and gently touched the brakes, pulling down as fast as he dared, easing off on the throttle simultaneously. The approaching car swelled up before them with almost frightening quickness.

Sergeant Lawe was set well back, but his eyes were closely on the car approaching. A red glow suddenly showed in the windshield approaching, and he said quickly, harshly: "Pull 'er down, boy, pull 'er down."

Clyde snubbed down hard then, in short, tire-squealing spurts, killing the momentum, foot down hard on the brake pedal now. The approaching car swung wide, onto the shoulder, ready to turn and pursue. Lawe snatched off his visored, badge-fronted cap and held it up above the windshield. Clyde pulled to a stop a few car lengths past the State Patrol car.

"Make a U-turn," said Lawe. He vaulted over the side, letting Clyde turn without him, ran to the State Patrol car. Clyde turned. Lawe leaned out the side of the State Patrol car and beckoned him on. "Follow us!" he bellowed.

Clyde waved. The State Patrol car leaped into motion, and he followed it easily. Once he grinned faintly. The State Patrol car sounded and acted like a strictly stock job. The cops could use some hopping-up, if that were the case. He could see Sergeant Lawe talking to the microphone through the rear window. Clyde checked his mirror. Nothing followed them.

At Lawe's car, nothing seemed changed. The second State Patrol car parked just short of it, on the wrong side of the highway, and Clyde was waved in behind it. Lawe came stalking, snatched the riot gun—a twelve-gauge pump shotgun, shortened in the barrel—from Clyde's car.

"Know how to shoot a rifle?" he demanded.

Clyde nodded.

Lawe caught up the lever-action rifle from the seat, showed him the working of the action. He pulled the badge from his own chest and stabbed the pin through Clyde's lapel. "You're deputized. Here's extra ammunition. You're guarding the cars. Get over in that ditch where you can cover 'em. If a scraggly-lookin' character comes out of the brush with a rifle, and doesn't drop it the second you say, you shoot him. Through the legs if you can, but through the belly if you have to. Don't take any chances. Don't get close to him. Fire a shot in the air in any case, so we'll know to come running. Now keep your head down and your eyes open."

"Where you going?" asked Clyde.

"Why," said Sergeant Lawe, as if in surprise, "we're going in after him . . . what the hell did you think?" He wheeled and ran, crouching, along the cars. His pockets bulged with heavy shells, and the other trooper, similarly outfitted with riot-gun and laden with ammunition, stepped out with him, glanced back once at Clyde, and then they both went at a steady, purposeful walk into the jumbled riot of brush that clogged the interstices here between taller timber. Within seconds there was not even sound of them to mark their going.

Clyde felt the cool, metallic weight of the rifle in his hands. He looked down at it, remembering that he'd have to cock the hammer before firing, found himself instinctively crouching as he ran across the macadam, took the sliding fall in a way he'd thought he'd probably forgotten since Army days, the forward-leaning, rifle angled butt down to catch part of his weight, the instant lifting and forward thrust to bring the barrel up into the sighting plane. He marveled at that a little, but his eyes never left off their careful sweep of the silent threat of the hiding brush across the way, and after a bit his breathing was normal, and aside from the aroused tingling of watchfulness he felt almost at home.

This wasn't bad. He was neatly kegged up; the borrow-pit was almost as secure as a good deep foxhole; he was open to enfilading fire from the sides, but the enemy numbered only one, and he could watch his flanks with fair security, for, if the killer did attempt to flank him, he'd have to cross the bare macadam to do it—and on the heels of that thought came the cold knowledge that he'd just possibly been mouse-trapped. The killer could have crossed the highway any time while they were gone. He could be behind him now, in the equally fine cover on this side of the highway—he could be drawing a bead on his back this instant. Clyde began to sweat.

He moved his head cautiously, swiveling his eyes in a slow, careful scanning of the length of the ditch that he could see. A hundred and fifty feet or so away, a tentacle-rooted stump lay capsized above the ditch, a remnant of a windfall the highway crew had bucked out of the way, probably. He eyed it, and decided, and then sprang up and ran toward it, crouching in the ditch, stumbling over the litter and rock in its rough bottom, and was gasping for air when he slid into the comparative safety of the thick wooden bulwark. With its massive shape at his back, he felt better, and after a minute's careful listening without hearing any sound of note he reached out and cleared a few weeds and an upthrust limb that interfered with his field of fire. Then he waited.

He thought about Sergeant John Lawe and the trooper who had gone into the brush after their man. It had been a very brave thing to do—walking into the killer's own chosen ground. The odds were far and away on the killer's side. He could move, or not, at his choice, with a multitude of hiding places and his choice of a thousand ambuscades. Two men couldn't comb. They could only pursue, and a clever man would leave little or no trail. It was a very chancy gambit in a very deadly game, and Clyde was glad that he was not more a part of it than he was now. He waited, and the time went very slowly.

He heard a car, coming at high speed along the highway. It made a sound of diminishing speed, coming into the curve and then burst into sight and pulled down quickly, another black State Patrol car that stopped and then ejected a pair of troopers, one from either side, who stared at the three parked cars, and then around. Clyde stood up and hailed them.

They wheeled on him with almost ludicrous quickness, wheeled crouching and ready and alarmed, one flinging up a riot gun to bear, the other hurling himself aside and clawing the revolver from his holster, that one shouting at him in a strained voice: "Drop it, mister! Drop that rifle right now!"

For just an instant Clyde hesitated, confused, and then said: "It's all right. I'm with the police. I'm Cameron. Sergeant Lawe left me here."

The one with the riot gun said: "Put it down. Step away from it."

Clyde carefully leaned the rifle against the weathered stump and moved away from it. He held his hands out from his sides. He wasn't as startled now, and he said: "All right. There are a dozen cards in my billfold. Press card in my breast pocket. Badge here on my lapel. Lawe said I was a deputy."—this last very dryly, seeing their watchfulness slightly relaxing. "Honest, fellas, I'm a good guy. I'm on your side."

They checked him out anyway—which was no more than sensible, Clyde admitted to himself. Then, satisfied as any cop will ever be with any taxpayer, the one with the riot gun said: "Where's Lawe and the other man now?"

Clyde pointed. "In there, some place. Been maybe ten, fifteen minutes, maybe more. I haven't been checking the time except the last few minutes."

They moved not quite uncertainly around the cars, looking into the brush which told them nothing at all. One of them said to the other: "What do you think, Pink?"

"Don't know," said the other one. "Captain coming?"

"On his way. What do you think?"

"Hell, we don't even know where they're at." This one looked around at Clyde, not really embarrassed, but somewhat uncertain. Then he cocked his head and said: "Bet that's him now."

He trotted across the highway, to be visible that much sooner to the car that was coming, waving as it burst into sight on the curve. The car stopped in a squealing of abused rubber, and the captain got out.

He looked at the troopers and at Clyde. "Where did you get that badge?"

"Sergeant Lawe deputized me," said Clyde.

"Where is he?"

Clyde told him.

The captain considered a moment, drew his pistol, and fired three spaced shots into the air. He stalked back to his car, unshipped his mike, got out a map, and began a steady, precisely spoken list of orders. Clyde drifted closer, shamelessly eavesdropping, watching the captain's finger as it shifted from point to point on the marked map, ticking off the instructions to his unseen listeners.

Once he paused for an acknowledgment, and a voice protested. The captain said icily: "You may tell him I do not care how he does it. I want men on those spots if he has to deputize every logger, rancher, or anyone else who knows the country and owns a rifle or a pistol or a shotgun. Now, I repeat . . . car one one seven proceed to. . . ."

Clyde saw Sergeant Lawe come quickly out of the brush, take the sloping climb up the embankment to the highway.

The other trooper appeared perhaps a hundred feet behind him. The sergeant dropped the riot gun from its ready position, hooked it on his arm, and gave Clyde a faint, grim smile and shook his head.

The captain finished his instructions. He looked at Lawe.

"Not a thing," said the sergeant.

"You're certain it was our man," said the captain.

"It was," said Sergeant Lawe. He beckoned and led them a short distance past his disabled car. The carcass of a yearling doe deer lay in the ditch.

"That was his bait," said the sergeant. "He crippled it, hamstrung it . . . see, that hind leg's tied into the brush with a hunk of wire. I was cruising slow and saw it dragging and crippling around, and I stopped. I looked out over the hood, with the door open, and reached in back for my rifle, and I don't think the bullet missed my head more than two inches. If I'd waited another second, reaching for the rifle, he'd have got me. His second shot went through the right-hand door there, and the third one went up front some place. Stopped the motor, anyway. I hit the dirt and shot up the brush, and ran him out, I guess. I put the deer out of its misery, and about that time Cameron came along. It was our boy, all right. I don't know whether he wanted me or the car, but he came close enough, either way."

"All right," said the captain unemotionally. He wheeled on the rest of them then, gave crisp orders, deploying the troopers up and down the highway.

They inspected the sergeant's car. The third, soft-nosed, high-powered rifle bullet had smashed the battery and resultant flying chunks from that explosive impact had knocked wires loose.

"We're wasting time," said the captain. "Cameron. Since you are deputized, you are under orders. Drive the sergeant to the resort, where he can get another battery. John, tell them I'll get a requisition to them later. Come directly to the command post when you get the car running. I'll want you to lead a party as soon as I can get it assembled."

The sergeant nodded, turned, and trotted to Clyde's car, Clyde following, not protesting. He wanted to get to the resort phone in any event. He had a story.

"Roll this heap," said Sergeant Lawe. "And if I ever catch you driving like this again, I'll send you up for life." He gave Clyde a thin, humorless grin, and Clyde rolled it.

The operational plan was as good as the sheer size and wildness of the country would allow. The triangle had been reduced by the efforts of Sergeant Lawe to a fractional corner, within which the killer was almost certainly confined. With that much likely the machinery went into motion. The black cars came rolling, everything that could be spared within a fifty-mile radius. A special squadron, previously *en route* from the State Headquarters, had already arrived. The county sheriff, arriving with two deputies, sent a message to the county seat for all uniformed personnel, and a county car brought all available badges and arm bands, plus arms, ammunition, folding tables, typewriters, cards, and files. Forest Service pickups and cars came scurrying. The logging companies' fire protection association sent men and field phones and portable radios, plus a field kitchen.

Highway 222 was sealed off from the resort access road to the command post, which was at the junction on an old logging road and 222. All fire look-out towers were alerted and reinforced with armed men, and the sketchy roads accessible from the highway were patrolled by men afoot and in jeeps and pickups. Field phones were tapped into the fire line at strategic intervals. Radios were set up at crossroads and high places. Men lined up and got their badges or armbands. The typewriters rattled out I D cards signed by the sheriff and the captain.

"If you don't know him," was the instruction, "don't trust the badge. Make him show the card. Don't be careless, but don't go trigger happy. Most of you boys know this country, and you know each other. Don't leave any vehicle with the motor running or the keys in it. Don't . . . for God's sake . . . shoot at noises. Anybody, armed or not, without a badge and I D card . . . hold him and call in. Now you go with this group here. . . ."

Emergency traffic went through the sealed section of 222 under escort, after each car had been carefully shaken down. Every vehicle to and from the resort, the summer homes, the camping areas on Sapphire Lake was stopped and checked. And long before all these sealing-off operations had been completed, Sergeant John Lawe took a uniformed ground party of twenty-three men into the brush in a long, sweeping skirmish line. This dragnet scanned the brush in carefully controlled sweeps.

It was too much of a job for twenty-three men. It was too much for a hundred. But they went in. Each man was uniformed for his own safety and positive identification. Every trooper carried a sawed-off shotgun and many extra buck-shot-loaded shells. The trap, the best they could contrive, was snapping shut.

The man went at his cautious stop-and-move gait after the first rapid retreat. He had run a steady half mile, after the big cop had started shooting back. Once he looked almost accusingly at the use-polished rifle in his hands. The sack slung at the back of his belt was slack and empty. He had cartridges and matches in his pockets; he had thoughtlessly wolfed the food retrieved from his cabin in a couple of prodigious meals. Now his half-starved body had but recently been well fed, almost gorged, and strength had come back to it, but he was hungry again, and he had not the self-discipline to ignore this. Like any wild animal, his wants were of the moment, insistent and urgent; he bore hardship with no patience at all, although what might have been near misery to another man was no hardship at all to him, for his wants were simple. But his wants were also urgent, and until he was satisfied he gave no thought to future needs at all.

He was not used to running over any great distance, and he was somewhat winded, and thirsty. He went almost directly to water, drank, went on a little way, and hid himself again. He had not slept a full night in twelve or thirteen days, although he made no real effort to assess the time accurately. He had slept in naps of an hour or two, sometimes three, when he was torpid of a full belly. He slept and prowled, and slept again, or sat simply hunched and watchful for hours on end.

He slept now and woke with an expression of disquiet, harking alertly without movement until some thought or alarm jelled within him. At last the sound came again, part of that which had been registered unconsciously to awaken him. His eyes almost closed. He raised his head, let his lips fall away from his teeth in a slack, feral grin, the breath stopping in his chest while he listened, and then he slid the rifle into balance in his hands and left the covert soundlessly, moving ahead of the sound.

Moments later, a doe, bedded perhaps a hundred feet downwind, got up, trampled softly about her bed, swiveled the great oval funnels of her ears at the distant sounds, and moved in her turn. She passed within forty feet of the man who had stopped, and was waiting out one of his pauses. He

slid the rifle forward, softly, easily, laid the sights on her neck, followed that plain and tempting target through three or four steps, then made a grimace of frustrated disgust and lowered the weapon. He shot a hateful, grinning look back at the on-coming sounds, and then moved on, resentfully, slowly, almost as if determining some nagging point in his thoughts.

He angled across the approaching skirmish line, evalu-ating with wild wisdom the numbers, the speed of their ap-proach, the length of the line. Then a shot bellowed out yonder, and his shoulders made an involuntary wincing shrug, and he made a headlong leap to shelter, landed sliding on knees and elbows and down-thrust rifle butt, froze there and waited while a distant voice murmured in chiding tones. Someone had fired an accidental shot. But he was sweating, before he decided on that, and little ripples of tension ran up his arms and across his wrists and the backs of his hands. He grinned his meaningless grin and felt fresh sweat running across his ribs. He squirmed and then moved on, more quickly now, but cautiously, trotting, sometimes where the few wide places allowed such motion, darting across them in almost a sidestep, with the rifle ready and his close attention on the approaching, threatening sounds. Once he reached up to cuff the sweat from his forehead, and only then noted that he had lost the lop-brimmed hat he had worn. He made a dis-gusted sound, but did not pause.

He moved more directly away from the sound, came on a long-reaching, silk-skinned windfall, the bleached wood bare of bark, the upthrust tentacles of its splayed roots almost buried in bronze-boled, gray-leafed manzanita. He placed a hand on the long-felled tree trunk, vaulted over it, crouched, and backtracked along it to the great upthrust root end, there went to cover again, hearing all sound now to his left, as if he had cleared the end of the approaching line.

Two roots crossed, leaving an oval aperture from which the earth had long since washed; in this aperture he laid the muzzle of the rifle. Nothing showed save that dismal, black-centered ring, and it was in shadow, so that the sun did not glint on the metal.

The end men of the line came into view, first as more patches of motion beyond the manzanita, then, once, a leg showed, as the man stopped a moment and listened, again to come forward, into a small space between trees clearly in the sun, a watchful, uniformed man, the badge on his chest, the insignia on his cap, glinting in the hot light, the sheen of clean, polished leather of boots and belt bright with its own light, the stout, powder blue cloth of the uniform clean and pressed. He stood there, the trooper, sending his eyes in quick, watchful sweeps, the riot gun cradled chest high, ready, waiting—eager perhaps, slightly tensing, it seemed, almost as if some unconscious thing told him of the nearness of the other. Then behind him came a softly murmuring voice: "O K, Sarge. Swing right. We got it."

This one came into view at the other's back; he had a compact handie-talkie slung over his shoulder. "We go right," he said, not much above a whisper. "Till we hit the dirt road. Then we notify Lawe."

"O K," said the first one. His eyes were swinging the length of the windfall, suspiciously scanning the breast-works and entanglements of stump and roots. Then the second man stepped past him, came between the small eye of the hidden rifle muzzle and the first man, went at a slow, trudging gait past the windfall with a cursory scanning of the length of it, trod almost precisely where the hidden man had stepped in crossing the downed tree, and went on, bearing to his right now, away from the windfall. A dozen strides took both troopers out of sight, and only the soft

sounds of their passage came back.

When even that small sign was gone, the man crabbed out of his ambuscade, bore left, and was swallowed into the shady cover as if he had never been.

He heard a grumbling jeep motor ahead, waited out its passing in complete immobility, and came then to the road. They had dragged it, hauled some pole or timber behind a machine to smooth and level the dust of the road. On that smooth surface a footprint would look like a monument. The man gave it a disgusted, sneering look and moved along the road edge a few yards to where a stone had stubbornly resisted previous travel and this new drag, stepped back and leaped, took the descending shock on one leg, the foot on the unheeding stone thrust strongly downward the instant his body came in line and leaped onward with only that thrust and his momentum, and the road was cleared without a trace of his passing. He did not even glance back to reassure himself of it.

He kept a steady course, thereafter, and a steady gait. A man following his footsteps might have thought it an erratic course, but it was not. He never climbed when he could go around. The brushy obstacles he slid through, edged through, disturbing the leaves and slender twigs only slightly, and within seconds of his passing there was no swinging motion, no turned leaf of bruised twig to mark his path. His feet lifted cleanly from the forest duff, not scuffing or dragging. It was tribute to the speed he made without seeming to extend himself that he came to the lower end of Sapphire Lake before dusk.

From the time he first sighted the glint of water, he moved with complete caution. He kept well back from the open beaches, slid from shelter to shelter in a quick, insistent rhythm. Finally he saw the man in the boat, just offshore, a bass fisherman casting into the weedy shallows, in a little bay almost hidden behind outthrust tongues of earth.

He scanned all the visible lake, the opposite shoreline, everything within his view, and then he raised the rifle, slid through the last screening brush, and trudged down to the lake shore. The man in the boat did not look up at once. He was busy and concentrated on his fishing. The killer stood a moment, a dour and watchful look coming on him, and then he lined the rifle and said in a nasal, carrying tone: "All right, bring that boat in here, mister."

The fisherman looked up then, startled. He located the man with the rifle, stared, and then swiveled his head in a quick, despairing look out over the lake. The man with the rifle pulled the hammer back in a double metallic click. It was plainly visible across the fifty feet of quiet water between them. "Bring it in," he said. "Don't you go to touch that motor."

The boat was drifting; it was not anchored. The fisherman took up one oar and used it as a paddle, bringing the boat slowly ashore.

"Git out."

The fisherman came out, leaning forward, supporting his hands on the gunwales cautiously, as a man should in a boat. He was a middle-aged man, not heavy, more than a little frightened, almost completely unsure. "Who are you?" he said. "What's the idea of that gun?"

"Turn around."

"I got nothing in my pockets except my tobacco and a handkerchief and some fishing stuff."

The rifle was raised, as if the barrel were a club. "Turn around!"

The fisherman turned. From that raised position the rifle barrel went back, over the killer's left shoulder. Then it shot

170

forward in a lunging butt stroke that drove the fisherman forward and off his feet with a sound like a thick, green limb breaking, as the butt plate smashed into the back of his neck.

The killer stood looking down at the limp, sprawled body with a slackly brooding expression. Once he put out a toe and nudged the nearest leg. He did not disturb the body otherwise.

He walked to the boat, stepped in, laid the rifle carefully braced between thwart and hull, took up the oar and shoved off. After working the boat out on the little bay, he stepped to the stern, carrying the rifle with him, fiddled with the small outboard a few moments, then started it, turned the boat, and boldly headed out into the lake, setting an angle course toward a section of the summer homes on the far shore. The boat moved smoothly and sedately and unhurriedly.

About a third of the distance from the foot of the lake, a short, sloping ridge thrust a narrow peninsula into the water. Beyond this ridge the summer homes were built; just below, a ramp for loading and unloading trailered boats; a public access point, one of three on the lake. Above the little peninsula, tucked into the bay it formed, was the Seaforth private dock, and the house above, one of the more choice summer homes. Tied in at the dock was a sleek inboard runabout, and an equally sleek little hydroplane, an outboard job, with its cockpit covered with snugly fitted canvas.

Kathy Cameron stirred restlessly in the canvas deck chair on the sunny patio. The Seaforth summer home was of Swiss-Alpine style, steep-roofed, brown-timbered; a square bite had been excavated against the hillside, and a rock retaining wall built to hold that shape on two sides; a lower stone wall gave a view of the lake, and a stone fireplace filled one corner. The footing was flagstones in a carefully fitted pattern, and at the corner of the house a flagstone walk continued around to the front terrace. Above the house was a graveled parking lot and below a series of short walkways, and steps led down to the beach and the dock. By virtue of its location and the angle of the ridge, it was secluded, screened by earth and trees, so that the only visible sign of the nearest other home was a mere glimpse of a roof peak above one shorter clump of trees. It was a quiet and secluded and lovely retreat, and still Kathy stirred restlessly, got up from her deck chair, strolled, almost pensively, to the flagged walkway, past the corner of the house, out to the front terrace.

She stood there a moment, staring unseeing out over the lake, finally folded her arms across her chest in a gesture of uncertainty or resignation, walked across the flagged terrace and back, her head tipped forward, watching without really seeing where her feet were going. Larry Seaforth had taken the car and gone somewhere; she thought to round up some people for a casual party tonight. Larry was doing his charming best to make sure of her enjoyment of people and parties. They had been fun until she had seen Clyde, and now she was alone and thoughtful, preoccupied and uncertain. She walked down to the dock, her hands behind her, head down; her slight figure might have been a child's figure at some slight distance, a pensive and thoughtful child, perhaps brooding over some small punishment. At closer range no one but a fool would have thought her a child, for, although she was small and neatly made, she was a woman, and a lovely one.

She stood on the deck and absently watched the boat approach—a small, green-painted fisherman's skiff—it was only when it was coming very close that she realized that it was coming in to the dock, and she gave it her first look of real curiosity. The man in the boat was young, rather darkly good-looking, but rough-looking; she assumed he was probably one of the campers who pitched tents and didn't look like anyone who might be a friend of Larry's. Larry's taste in friends didn't run much to those likely to rough it in tents. Probably it was someone who just wanted to ask a question or tie up a few moments while he tinkered with his motor. At any rate the boat came on, the young man watching her but not waving or calling out, watching her while he ran in close, cut the motor with a chop of his hand, and reached out and grasped a trailing line at the dock, hooked it over a cleat in the stern, and then stepped out, all in one motion, not making any move to pull in the bow, although the boat swung at his debarking push and then rocked back to bang the exposed outboard motor against the dock edge.

She had quite thoughtlessly assumed that it was a cased fishing rod he took from the boat—she saw now that it was a rifle, and twinge of alarm went through her, and she said: "What do you want? This is a private dock, you know."

The man smiled thinly, a pale flashing of yellowed teeth against his dark skin. "Honey," he said, "you turn around and walk. Right up to the house."

"Who are you?" she demanded. "What do you want?"

His eyes bent over her, and her alarmed uncertainty deepened. "You'd better get out of here," she said, "before I call for help to put you off."

He advanced two prowling steps, and she made herself stand fast before him. "Honey," he said in a voice oddly strained, but quiet, "did you ever see what a soft-nosed bullet would do to one of them pretty legs? Don't you open your mouth. You just turn around like I said an' walk. Who's up at the house?"

She stared at him, suddenly remembering. Larry was gone. There wasn't anyone at the house. For a moment a small panic overtook her. It must have showed on her face.

The man said in a satisfied tone: "That's good. Nobody around, huh? All right, move, honey. Or do I have to move you?"

The rifle muzzle slid out. She winced at the cold, metallic touch of it against her bare leg. Suddenly shaken, she turned, unable to think of anything else to do, and led the way up the walkway, a few steps up, another walk, more steps. She could feel his eyes on her, and suddenly wished she was wearing something besides shorts and blouse. She wished—she wished desperately—that Larry would come, that anyone would come. Quite suddenly, she was truly frightened.

Clyde swung the convertible in at the resort service station, left Sergeant Lawe to arrange for a new battery, and trotted to the resort lodge. From the lobby phone he called in his story to the *Register*, giving a rapid-fire summary of fact without attempting to embellish it with color. At this stage of the game it was strictly bulletin material, and he made no attempt to dictate polished prose.

He finished that hurriedly, promised a follow-up at the first chance, and ran, urged on by an impatient outcry from his car horn under the heavy hand of the sergeant. He told the man at the gas pumps to alert Ray Courtney, got a promise that the man would notify the resort desk, the dock attendants, and anyone else that Courtney would likely see, and then Clyde drove the sergeant back to his car.

They were still at the business of installing the battery when Ray arrived in his own car. Ray got pictures of them at work, a shot of the bullet holes in the car, and then fell in as they went in convoy to the command post.

Ray shot pictures with abandon and howled like a trapped wolf when they wouldn't let him go into the brush with the sergeant's ground party. Clyde interviewed the sheriff and some of the deputized civilians, managed to promote a circling jeep ride with one of the deputies around the perimeter of the besieged area, then came back to the command post. There wasn't much else to do but wait.

Captain Carrington allowed him to use one of the field phones tapped into the outside line, and Clyde dictated a follow-up, a recap of what he'd had before, and promised more as things developed. Then it was wait; monitoring the radio hookup, the jingling field phones; pacing up and down, smoking, chatting, getting names and statements which might be of use later for a big story—hell, there would be only one big story: the capture or killing of the killer. By midafternoon, it began to shape up to the rather dull certainty that there wasn't going to be any big story. The sergeant's skirmish line swept the area, combed it in long sweeps, with one end anchored, and the line pivoted on that, and then another with the first pivot, making its own sweep.

They routed deer from their beds. Innumerable chirping, chattering, scampering little wild things flushed out under their feet. Once a skulking coyote, temporarily trapped or thinking he was, burst through the line in a frantic, zigging run, bringing a joyous yip from one of the troopers and a lashing-down from the sergeant that left the trooper scarlet-faced and shocked. But they did not find their man. Clyde was at the field set when the faint word came from one of the handie-talkies: "We're bearing in on the section. No sign." That was it. That was the last still uncombed.

The sweep went through, and then back, almost desperately, as if the many searching men could not believe their own senses. The killer was gone. He had vanished—up a tree, down a hole—and yet the party would swear individually and collectively that they had investigated every hole, shaken every tree. The bald fact remained. The killer was still at large.

Sergeant Lawe was the last man to come out of the brush. The high polish was gone from his boots; the legs were welted and scratched where they had been forced through stubborn brush; his breeches were stained by the countless leaves and twigs they'd brushed; but it was in keeping with what Clyde knew of the man that his uniform blouse was still buttoned, that his visored cap sat square on his close-cropped head, that his back was still straight and his shoulders square. Only his trudging gait showed the deep tiredness in him. He shook his head at the captain, gave Clyde a nod, and then spotted the field kitchen mounted on the truck standing by, and walked to it. He got a cup of water from the white-aproned man in charge, drank that down, then unloaded the riot gun, dumped the shells in his pocket, stripped off gun belt and blouse and caught a trickle of water from one of the spigoted water tanks and scrubbed his sweaty face and head with wet hands.

The captain said: "No sign at all?"

"We found his hat," said the sergeant. He reached into his blouse and brought out a crumpled wad of black felt that, when shaken out, fell into a semblance of a hat. "We found where he'd kegged up. I'll swear he was in there, but we never saw hide, hair, or tracks. He's in there . . . he's got to be in there!"

"How do you know it's his hat . . . or that it wasn't lost a week ago?"

The sergeant dropped the limp hat. It fell crown downward, resting in a crumpled segment of the brim. It continued a slow-motion collapse. "That's why," said the sergeant. "Let that lay a half a day, and it'd be flat on the ground as a rug. It wasn't when we found it. Where he'd kegged up, the needles were stirred. They hadn't bleached dry yet. He's in there. I ought to have more men to go in after him."

The captain said musingly: "If he was really trying to escape, skip out, we'd pick him up with road blocks and patrols. An ordinary man wouldn't last in there. We'd starve him out or freeze him out or dry him out. Not this one. Unless we heard him shoot a deer . . . and you know how this timber deadens sound . . . he can eat. An ordinary man would be all crippled up after three nights of sleeping on the ground. He's been in there twelve, and he's still going strong. He knows where there's water. He's doing all right by doing it all wrong, and we still haven't laid eyes on him."

"No," said the sergeant. "What do we do . . . write it off, or just sit on our thumbs?"

Some of his irritation and tiredness came through on those words, and the captain eyed him sharply, seemed almost to speak, and then did not. He stood erect, not moving his hands as a man almost always does when thinking, once made a little grimace at some thought, and said finally: "We'll get him, John, you know that. But we can't assume he's in there, not any more."

"Then somebody let him get by. I think he's still in there. I just didn't have enough men . . . to look in every hole and up every tree."

"Where are you going to get more men? We can't wait for troops, even if the governor would turn them out."

"Then we've got to go in after him again now, with whatever we've got."

"Maybe. After I've satisfied myself. I'll cover the perimeter myself. Then I'll decide."

"It'll be dark by then."

The captain looked at him. "Probably," he said.

The sergeant let out a long sighing breath and turned away.

The captain said in a quieter voice: "Get something to eat, John. We'll get him."

"Sure, captain," said Sergeant Lawe tonelessly. "Eventually."

Clyde waited until the sergeant had got a plate of food and a cup of coffee from the truck kitchen. He sat down beside him. "How is it in there?" he asked.

"Rough," said Sergeant Lawe.

"Think you could have missed him? That he could have slipped through your line?"

"He could, yes. I looked back once, and a buck deer got up and sneaked off. Laid right there, while a man walked by on each side. Didn't have enough men for a tight line with any swing to it." He chewed, swallowed, and put his fork down. He put out a hand that trembled slightly. "I'm tired," he said bluntly, "but I'm scared, too. I was scared every second I was in there. Just waiting for the shot . . . that meant he'd got somebody. Oh, they'd get him . . . somebody on one side or the other. But he'd get somebody first . . . maybe two of 'em, before the buckshot hit him. Maybe he isn't wound up tight enough to try it yet, but he will be, and it'll get worse, the longer it goes. He's going to kill himself another cop if we don't nail him down quick. I'd rather go in there alone than take those boys in with me. But I couldn't push him alone, and some of these boys think it's a kind of exciting game. I know him, and it's no game. He'll kill somebody if we don't nail him quick."

"But you think he's still in there?"

The big sergeant put his plate aside. He drank the hot coffee almost greedily. "I don't know," he said finally. "I don't know." He sat tiredly, looking at the ground.

It was well toward sunset before the captain returned from

his inspection. "No sign he did, no sign he didn't," he replied to Clyde's question. He turned away then and started issuing his crisp instructions. It was his intention apparently to seal off the area for the night, for he wanted trucks, jeeps, cars, spotlights placed where they could command certain stretches of the perimeter with their light, and there were to be in addition riding and foot patrols on overlapping beats. Clyde found Ray Courtney.

"I've got my story out," he said. "But one of us ought to be here, in case anything breaks. You want to stand by and have me relieve you later?"

"O K. Bring some more flash bulbs when you come. They're in my room."

Clyde showered, in his room, changed to a pair of knock-about slacks and a flannel shirt, and got out the portable. He hammered it steadily for an hour, knocking out his lead story, giving it depth and color, worked out half a dozen shorter items, interviews, personality stories on various posse members, then took the sheaf of papers downstairs and got the *Register* desk and dictated the entire thing *verbatim*. He answered the last query and left the phone booth, feeling oddly let down and purposeless.

He wandered about the lobby, saw the clerk putting the out-of-town edition of the *Register* on a wire rack, and got one. Down at the bottom of the front page was a two-paragraph story headed—**KILLER STILL AT LARGE**—that was merely a resumé of the killing of Trooper McVey and the fruitless hunt since. Due to the time lag, this down-state edition was a full day behind and carried none of Clyde's copy. In the city, that news was already on the streets, and the edition now *en route* here would carry the same stories. It gave Clyde a queer, disjointed feeling after being accustomed to working on the city edition.

He was restless. He looked in on the dining room and was not hungry. He sat in the lobby and knew he should be catching a nap, for likely he'd stay with the thing all night, once he went back out to the area of the search. He thought of Kathy, and tried to dismiss that thought and leaned back in the chair, and the thought came again, and he sighingly took it in and examined it, and the conclusion suddenly came to him that he was a damned fool. Brave words, indeed: *learn to live with it*. He wasn't learning. He'd given into a thing of finality, and then could not persuade himself that it was final. He thought of a good many things—the good times and the bad ones—he thought of Kathy in Larry Seaforth's hands, and a feeling of pure red outrage was on him. He had evaded the thought, but he walked into it now, pulled it apart, and watched it go back together—examined it from all sides.

He had given her up, and still he had not. He had simply not made any effort to stop her. He had been almost completely passive in the matter, and now for the first time felt a touch of anger at himself for doing so. Maybe it had been a sort of numbness at first, an outrage of his own pride, that she should want to leave him—*could* want to leave him—an outrage so great that he could not bring himself to fight it. He rubbed his hands together and found them damp and trembling.

He examined himself most carefully then. He wasn't pitying himself, and he had to assure himself of that. It wasn't as simple as the biological result of a month of loneliness. Nor could he find a feeling of self-righteousness. He knew his own faults and where a portion of the blame lay. Nor was he defending himself with a remorsefulness that took all the blame and conjured up a perfection or rightness to Kathy's actions. The plain and simple truth was that he hadn't tried hard enough—*they* hadn't tried hard enough—that regardless of what had happened before or since, he couldn't let it lie there now—he could not possibly accept it a moment longer. That much he knew.

He went down to the dock and got the boat he and Ray had used in fishing, cast off, and set out across the lake, the outboard throatily growling at full throttle.

It wasn't simple. He did not attempt to fool himself with that one. Cut it as thin as you liked, there was still Larry Seaforth, and all the past unresolved. What she would think or do—or even the little item of whether anything of her own resolution might have changed—all this was still a part of the problem, and the only difference in it now lay in his own resolve that he could no longer endure passively. The boat seemed damnably slow. He saw none of the beauty of sunset over the lake as he crossed.

He saw that another green-painted resort boat was tied in at the Seaforth dock—sloppily tied in, so that the boat streamed out at right angles to the dock and banged the motor on the little watery back-surges. Not thinking about it particularly, he tied his own boat, and, because he was of that methodical type, he caught the bow painter of the other boat and tied it, too. Then he ascended toward the house.

He thought he saw someone at the screened doorway that opened on this side of the house. He walked on, not letting himself feel anything in particular. It didn't really matter who it was. Then he heard the crunch of tire on the winding graveled driveway that led down from the access road above, saw the car come into view on the lot beyond the house, saw that Larry Seaforth was the driver, and had a dismal feeling that he had missed an opportunity to see Kathy alone. He looked back to the screened doorway, at the indistinct figure inside, a man's shape.

It didn't come to him for a moment. He had been accustomed to seeing men armed with rifles as a matter of course lately. But suddenly he was aware that this man was armed, that his pose showed a watchfulness, and sickeningly a certainty came on him. He had found the killer.

He fought the thought. It was wild. It was preposterous. And somehow it was undeniable. Out of the clamorous confusion inside him, some reasonable being seemed to direct his movements. He did not stare at the doorway, or give any sign of seeing anyone. He stopped, looked down blankly, flipped a hand in the manner of a man who has forgotten something, and turned back toward the dock. He could hear the boom of the car door closing. Then a quick, chilling voice called: "Come back here, you!" He knew then.

He turned, as a man might, at a call of no particular importance.

The screen door swung out, pushed by an outthrust foot, and the rifle was plainly visible then, lined on his middle. "Come on," said the voice.

Larry Seaforth came around the corner of the house and walked right into it. The rifle muzzle swung on him at a distance of no more than ten feet, and the chilling voice said: "Get over there, damn you!" It gestured toward Clyde, and Larry's head swiveled that way, his eyes recognized Clyde, and he blurted: "What the hell . . . ?"

Clyde said swiftly—"Better do it, Larry."—and the voice inside said: "God damn you . . . jump! I'd just as soon blow your guts out as not!"

Larry's face went white with shock. His head turned left and right, from the gun to Clyde, and back again. His mouth shakily formed the words. "What . . . what . . . ?" but he moved, slowly, dazedly, at the rifle's commanding motion.

The voice said: "Come in . . . come in. Don't make any

sudden moves. Come easy."

They went in. Easy. Clyde caught the edge of the screen door as it was thrust at him, held it, and walked through. At the unspoken command of the twitched rifle muzzle, he stood aside for Larry. The killer backed slowly away. He held the rifle with its stock tucked under his right elbow, and his left hand was clamped on Kathy's wrist, moving her with him with an easy, wiry strength. "Honey," he said without looking at her, "who are these two? Boy friends?"

Clyde felt himself shaking. She looked so fragile and vulnerable with one slim, white arm in the dirty, dark, grasping hand. He trembled in his restraint of the driving desire to charge that deadly weapon and tear her from him, trembled because he knew he must hold that restraint or die uselessly. Still that driving desire ate at him, and he could not stop trembling. But he held it, and said nothing.

Larry Seaforth wasn't accustomed to being spoken to in such a fashion. Shock had held him this long, but the words that burst out now were those of Larry Seaforth who just didn't put up with such things. He said: "Now you look here, mister . . . you get out of here right now, or you're going to find yourself in some real trouble!"

For just a tiny fraction of a second, Clyde thought it was coming. The dirty, dark hand tightened on the grip of the rifle until the knuckles paled. The hammer was cocked, and the forefinger tightened on the trigger. A blazing light seemed to keep behind the wild, lackluster eyes. Then the tight scratching voice said with deadly violence: "Pretty boy, you shut that damned mouth 'fore I shut it for you!"

It cut through Larry's righteous indignation as if cold edged steel had touched his throat.

"Trouble?" said the snarling voice. "You're the one's got trouble . . . you shoot off that mouth again. Git over there, pretty boy, or I blow your brains all over the wall!"

Still shocked, Larry moved. But he moved slowly, as if with contempt, unable to give in to what he detested. But he moved. Clyde went with him, not bucking it.

"That's better. So's we got a understandin'. Now, I got me a pretty little cook here, 'n' I don't want you boys to go spoilin' my supper. Just do like you're told. Now, honey. . . ."

Kathy had not moved. Her eyes were wide, and her lips trembled. Now as he spoke, she wrenched herself away in one strong, twisting pull, wheeled away from him in an almost panicky swiftness, snatched open the door behind her, and slammed it after her. Almost the rifle went off then. With a look of raw, wild violence, the killer leaped backward, even in this amount of stress keeping his restraint on Clyde and Larry. He crashed the steel butt plate of the rifle twice against the door, hard, and his eager whine called: "I count three, honey, and I shoot your pretty college boy right through the belly! Come out of there, 'cause I'm goin' to do it!"

He harked, but only for a second. "One," he said. "Two." The rifle was lined on Larry's belly, steady as a rock. The forefinger tightened.

Nothing in Larry Seaforth's life had ever prepared him for this. Probably his wildest dreams had never contained this sort of threat, real or imagined. Never had he faced such completely careless deadliness. And Larry Seaforth, scion and heir apparent to Seaforth, Inc., cracked wide open. His voice came out in a terrified shriek: "For God's sake, Kathy, do what he says! Kathy, *for God's sake!*"

The doorknob turned, with a soft, almost inaudible sound, and the killer threw a shoulder against it, drove it open against Kathy's half-hearted blocking. "Come out. Don't try me again on that one. Next move you make like that, I blow the brains out of both of them, an' then I come find you. That's the way you want it, you just try that one again. Now, you two . . . you, pretty boy . . . set down."

Larry was shaking. He could never retrieve that wild, despairing cry of utter, ignominious terror, and likely he would never forget it. He shook and trembled, as a man in a terrible chill of sickness. He looked sick, deathly sick, sick and despairing. He sat down, collapsed almost, onto the settee behind him. Clyde sat beside him.

This was the breakfast room end of the enormous kitchen. At their backs, behind the settee, were windows overlooking the lake. The kitchen end of the room was partially separated by a peninsular bar for serving casual meals. There was also a table, comfortable chairs, clever prints dealing with cookery and eating on the walls.

With his hip and the backs of his thighs, the killer shoved the table across the waxed linoleum floor. He kicked a chair around, put one foot on its seat, and set his buttocks on the table. He could command the entire room with a short sweep of his eyes now.

"All right, honey," he said. "I'm damn' hungry. You cook us somethin' to eat."

Kathy stared at him stonily, showing nothing but a taut watchfulness on her face.

"Honey," he said softly, "don't make me bust that pretty face to prove I mean business."

"What do you want?" she said stiffly.

"You cook it. I'll eat it. Just make plenty of it, and make it hot."

She turned without a word and went behind the bar, stood a moment, and then went to the refrigerator. Like the suspended globe lights, it was run by bottled gas. She pulled out dishes and put them on a worktable beside the stove.

"What d'you think you're goin' to do with that knife, honey?"

Kathy said evenly: "I'm going to slice this ham with it. Do you want something to eat, or don't you?"

In that moment Clyde was almost ridiculously proud of her. She had broken and run, and naturally enough from that first revulsion of the man's hand on her. She wasn't breaking now. She wasn't giving an inch now, and he was proud of her.

"Just so's you don't get any funny ideas, honey," said the killer softly. "Just you use it, an' then lay it out where I can see it plain."

She gave him a cold look of unforgiving aloofness, sliced ham, lighted the gas stove, put the ham in a skillet, and set it to cooking. She went again to the refrigerator for eggs, cracked them, and dumped them into the pan with the sizzling ham. She stood with her back to the man, rigidly hating him with her very posture. Once she looked around quickly, then back. The sound of frying ham was loud in the quiet room.

She picked the heavy skillet off the stove and turned toward the table finally. Clyde shifted his feet soundlessly.

The killer's voice said in a whip crack of sound: "Hold it, honey! Set it back. Git a plate and put it in there. Bring it over and set it down on the table. Now you wouldn't get any bright ideas about burnin' me with that scaldin' grease, would you? No, 'course not. Now you git over there an' set down with them two where I can keep an eye on you."

Clyde sighed soundlessly and let himself relax. If Kathy felt defeat, it did not show. She put the plate of food on the table and walked steadily toward the settee.

The killer watched her from behind appreciatively. Kathy gave that no sign, either. Her eyes came on Clyde, wide and searching, and he gave her a wry little smile. She looked at

186

Larry closely, unreadably. Then she shifted a trifle as she walked, to sit beside Clyde, so that Clyde was between her and Larry. She sat down primly, straight-backed, put her hands on her bare knees, and looked straight ahead, at the opposite wall.

The killer grinned cruelly, humorlessly laid the rifle atop the table, muzzle pointed at the settee. The hammer was still cocked, the grip and action not six inches from his right hand. He ate like an animal, snatching and chowing and gulping, never more than a quick, darting glance leaving them to see the food on the plate, only that quick, flicking motion lifting the weight of his watchfulness for even fractions of a second.

He ate it all, two thick slices of ham, four eggs; there was a basket of soda crackers on the table, and he ate all of those. He finished and belched and wiped his sleeve, his left sleeve, across his lips. He worked his lips and tongue around against his teeth in a scrubbing motion, grimacing in a way that made the spikes of his two-weeks' beard move in squirming undulation.

"Y'god," he said, "that helped. You c'n cook fer me anytime, honey."

Visibly, he was relaxed. He leaned back in the curved-backed captain's chair, and there was an easier, slacker expression on his face. But his hand lay almost touching the cocked and ready rifle. He said almost lazily, his eyes running over them: "You're a fine god-damn' bunch."

So might an Apache have looked down in contempt at his staked-out victim. So might a wolf, not quite famished with hunger, look at the hamstrung calf he had brought down. With contempt and some slight watchfulness and a complete possessiveness.

He said to Clyde: "What you doin' here. What made you come here?"

"Just came over to see these people," said Clyde without emphasis.

"Who owns this place? You, pretty boy?"

"It's . . . it's mine . . . my father's. You've got no right. . . ."

The killer made a grimace and looked away. "This your girl, pretty boy?"

"Yes . . . no . . . she's . . . well . . . he's her husband."

The wolfish eyes flicked at Clyde. "Some husband. Lettin' her run with pretty boy. Christ, I don't blame her, though . . . maybe she's lookin' for a real man. Sure made a mistake on pretty boy, didn't you, honey?"

Kathy did not change expression or look at him. She kept her level glance on the wall opposite.

Again the killer grimaced. "You got a car, pretty boy?"

"Yes."

"We'll use it . . . . after dark. You can be my driver." His eyes swung back to Kathy, and a tiny dancing flame began to shine behind his eyes. "Honey," he said, "I'm beginnin' to wonder if you're worth a damn for anythin' besides cookin'. Come over here, honey. Maybe we c'n find some place to lock these boys up for a while."

Clyde felt Kathy's sudden trembling. She did not look at the man, but her face whitened, and a tiny muscle jumped along her jaw line. Her knuckles whitened in their grip on her knees. She did not move.

"Come on, honey," said the man softly. His hand slid across the small of the rifle stock; his fingers slid, three through the metal loop of the lever action, the forefinger into the trigger guard.

Clyde said in a normal conversational tone: "No. Don't try that, Roy."

The wolfish snarl was suddenly focused, hard and bitter against him. "Well," he said, "another big mouth. What d'you think you'll do about it, big mouth?"

"I'm just saying it, Roy . . . don't try it. You'll have to kill me, if you do." He heard the sucking intake of breath of Larry beside him, felt the slight cringing motion transmitted through the cushions on which they both sat. He did not look at him. He kept his eyes on Roy, wracking his brain for the right words, the proper words, hoping he wouldn't stumble onto one of the trigger words unthinkingly. It was as wildly chancy as trying to pick a winning hand out of the fluttering mass of a deck of cards thrown into the air.

Roy said softly, deadly, impatiently: "Don't think I won't, mister. I'll kill you like stompin' a bug. You make a move an' see."

Clyde had interviewed perhaps a hundred of them. Talked with them, listened to them, gotten his stories from them, some of them handcuffed in police cars or raging behind bars. Once he'd helped talk one out of a barricaded room with an arsenal at hand. Raving maniacs, some of them, others seemingly as normal as any Joe Blow on any main street. So long as they didn't hear the wrong words—the trigger words. So frantically Clyde searched, not allowing that franticness to show, and said in an ordinary tone: "You're too smart for that, Roy. You've had plenty of chances to kill us, but you're too smart to do it unless you have to. There are a dozen houses within shouting distance. You fire a shot, and somebody will come. They know you're around, and they'll be nervous. Some of them will have guns, and then you'll have to shoot your way out, and that's just what you don't want. You wait for dark and pull out quietly, and you've got a good chance."

The killer was watching him with a close, deadly attention—but he was listening. "Big mouth," he said. "Big brain. So what the hell's it to you how I kill a little time before dark? You think I'm scared to pull this trigger on you, big mouth?"

"Not scared, smart. Play it steady and smart. Don't make it so you have to kill me." He didn't feel brave, saying it; resigned, perhaps, but not completely resigned, for he could taste his own fear; and he could not let it show.

The wolfish eyes flicked back and forth over the three of them. "Big mouth," he said again. "All I do is tie you up and ram your own socks in your big mouth."

"To do that you kill me, too. Not quiet and easy. You've got to shoot me. And then the neighbors come running with guns. No, you're too smart for that, Roy." Clyde made his hands lie relaxed on his thighs. He pressed himself on the cushioned back of the settee, but he could feel the dampness of his palms, the prickle of sweat at his hairline, the deep, thudding pulse in his throat.

To show his unconcern he shrugged his shoulders in the slightest of gestures, pulled his eyes away from the killer's, looked at Kathy. Her head turned slowly, and her eyes dark and large and full of some intangible emotion looked deeply into his. The strict stiffness of her lips was fading to a softness as she looked at him. He gave her an impersonal little smile, yearning to reach out to touch her impersonally under the watching eyes of the killer.

The killer said with a sullen indifference: "You talk too much, big mouth."

Clyde's inwardly cringing, cowardly body anticipated the bullet in that instant, but he held the slow rhythm of his breathing, turned his head slowly, not too slowly, toward the killer. The relief that came on the heels of the fearful anticipation was almost as much the undoing of his self-control as the other, but he held it.

Roy Tollifer had shoved himself slightly back from the table. He was looking at them, lax-faced, broodingly, but the tense threat was gone. His face was slightly flushed, seemed almost to have gained some slight puffiness. He'd bought it. Like a gorged animal, he had seemingly gone into a digestive somnolence, not indifferent, but not quite so threateningly alert. There was no telling how long this waiting period would last—what new unpredictability would come to his restless mind—but for now it was a time of waiting.

Dusk came creeping. The terrace, the patio, the walls of the house, all were in shadow. Light still blessed treetops high above, and, on the far shore of the lake, shafts of late sunlight thrust long blunt lances into the undergrowth. This Clyde could see vaguely in the mirror made by the angled-open, glass-windowed kitchen door. Out on the lake a few boats still plied, late fishermen heading homeward, a few diehards still trolling, and the late-evening bass fisherman not yet ready to give up at all. The sounds of motors came, softened by distance to gentle powder-puff touches of sound; somewhere, not too far away at other summer homes, children played and shrieked and laughed. These sounds were plain, but softened by the filtering of intervening trees. Somewhere a radio played an incongruous, bouncy jump tune. A heavy throbbing boat motor advanced across the lake. Above on the hidden roadway a car passed, growling in second gear. The killer harked to that sound alertly, relaxed as the sound continued and diminished.

Clyde felt the subtle relaxing of Kathy's body close to his. He felt a touch on his outer thigh, soft as a falling feather, and let his own hand slide down. For a moment her hand lay motionless beneath his, and then it stirred, and her fingers closed on his. He did not look at her, but a great, aching bubble began to rise in his chest. He looked down at his own knees, feeling absurdly that Roy Tollifer might be able to read something in his face. Suddenly his throat felt dry, and he swallowed. Her fingers on his gave just the slightest of pressures, and then relaxed. Out on the lake, he was dimly aware that the heavy throbbing boat motor sound was coming closer. Beside him, Larry Seaforth sat motionless.

Suddenly he knew that the killer was aware of the motor sound. It came with a lifting glance out through the windows behind them, the sudden galvanic alertness of the single, sweeping lift of the rifle from the table. The motor sound chopped off short, and a surging, splashing, washing sound drifted up from the deck. A shock of mingled relief and alarm cut through Clyde like a thin, edged blade.

"By God," said the killer, in a taut whisper. "By God!"

He came up from behind the table, the somnolent, waiting patience gone into a crouching, prowling awareness. His eyes were widened, and the slackness was gone from his expression. His wild look came on them all as hot as a lashing whip, and he said in a tight snarling tone that brooked no restraint: "Honey, get over to that door. Don't touch it . . . just stand there. You move, and the bullet gets him just the same. Only it goes through you first. Don't make me do it, honey!"

Kathy's fingers clutched convulsively on Clyde's. He gave her a replying pressure, meant to be reassuring. He turned his head and looked clearly at her, saw the questioning, pleading in them, gave her a slight smile. Gently he released his hand. She kept that look on him for only a tiny moment more, then stood, and walked to the door without looking at the killer. Clyde could not see well now; Kathy's shape, seen through the glass panels of the door, destroyed the mirror effect. He thought he caught a glint—perhaps it was only a flick of motion, a swatch of color that faded almost before he identified it. He looked at the killer, who had risen from the table, moved slightly aside. A ten-inch swing of the muzzle would cover the door or the settee at will.

Clyde gathered himself very carefully, tensing muscles

without visible motion, slightly and soundlessly shifting his feet. The hand Kathy had held soundlessly sank into the cushion for purchase.

Footsteps sounded outside on the flagged walk, solid, confident strides. Clyde could see the glint then, and the color, and knew he had not been mistaken, and he gathered himself as the killer's full attention went to the doorway and the man beyond it. Then Sergeant John Lawe's impersonal, professional voice said—"Ma'am, have you seen Clyde . . . ?"—and the killer's voice rode over that with: "Go ahead, cop, draw that god-damn' gun! Go on, damn you. I'd love for you to pull it!"

There was only that fraction of a second of time. Clyde surged up. Larry Seaforth fell into him frantically, a barring arm across Clyde's chest, a coarse, raw-throated whisper torn from him: *For God's sake, Cameron! For God's sake, don't!*

The instant was gone, then. The killer flicked only one flashing glance at that small struggle, took a short step aside, and Clyde almost prayerfully braced himself for the blasting of the shot, but the whispering voice of the killer said: "*Somebody* gets it if you move, cop! I don't care who!"

John Lawe said calmly: "All right, Roy. Nobody's moving."

"Come in then," said Roy. "Git out of the way, pretty girl. Hands up, cop. I'd just love to bust you."

John Lawe came in, big, bulky, showing nothing on his strong cop's face. He raised his hands, shoulder high.

"Pretty girl," said the killer in a taut, singing tone, "you unbuckle his belt. Move away. Remember, cop, she's little enough that the bullet'd go clean through her an' still git you."

"I'll remember," said John Lawe. He made no move while Kathy struggled with the heavy leather belt, found the Sam

Browne's fastening, and loosed that, too.

"Drop it," said the killer, and the heavy belt and accouterments made a double thumping sound on the floor.

"Might as well give it up, Roy," said John Lawe. "We've got you surrounded. Let these people go, and we'll talk it out from there."

A shrieking, high-pitched laugh came from the killer's throat. "Don't try to snow me, cop. I seen you come . . . alone. I'm wise to you cops and your bluffs. Ain't nobody with you, and, if they was, you'd be the first one to git his brains blowed out!" He kicked a chair away from the table. "Right over there at the end of that sofy. Set down."

Sergeant John Lawe pushed the chair into line with a booted foot and seated himself, lowered his arms to rest on the chair arms.

"Git them handcuffs, honey," said the killer. "Cuff the big cop to pretty boy . . . through the arm of the sofy. I'd love to watch 'em jump me draggin' that with 'em."

As Clyde had found long ago, averageness could be a blessing and a disguise. John Lawe was an obvious threat to the killer. Larry Seaforth was big and rangy and athletically built. In that quick side glance the killer hadn't been able to see who was tussling with whom. The cuffs made a scratching, ratcheting sound on Lawe's left wrist and Larry's right. Kathy stepped back at the gesturing barrel and sat again by Clyde. The killer came prowling, a taut and feral grin showing his teeth.

"You big bastard," he said to John Lawe. "I been achin' to see you in a fix like this all my life." He came forward almost carelessly, reached down, and clicked the cuff tighter by another notch. Without moving his body, John Lawe's big right fist came around. Like a striking snake, the seemingly carelessly held rifle barrel fell. Something snapped, a dull, greenbranch-breaking sound, and a grunt of pain came from the big policeman. His right arm fell, bent crookedly between wrist and elbow.

"Smart cop," jeered the killer. "Real smart cop. Think you know all the tricks. Go on, hit me with that busted wing. Wanna try for two? Smart cop!" He raised the rifle casually, rammed a brutal butt stroke into John Lawe's belly. The big man doubled up sickly. "Tough bastard, ain't you, cop?" He wheeled suddenly, wheeled and raked them all with the threat of the gaping rifle muzzle. "That's a small dose. I been playin' nice. You can all have some if you want."

John Lawe said sick-voiced, gaspingly: "Big mistake, Roy. Better . . . let these . . . people go. You're in trouble, boy."

Again that hideous laugh came. "Who's in trouble, cop? *Who's* in trouble? Five minutes, cop, an' I'll be long gone. Five minutes, an' pretty boy's goin' to drive me out of here, and maybe pretty girl will go along just for leverage. Maybe she'll like it. . . . You got maybe five minutes, cop, to think about how maybe you should have took up some other way to make a livin' . . . 'cause you ain't goin' to be livin' after that. I always loved to hear a big bear squeal when you stick him."

He moved back toward the table then, still holding them under the loosely held gun. He bounced the table with his hip, oriented himself by that, the rifle muzzle held high enough to clear the top of the bar if he wanted to fire, groping behind him for the knife that Kathy had laid in plain sight at previous order. He found it, and then came forward, grinning savagely, watching their faces with a curious eagerness, drinking in the expressions he found on their faces.

"Cop," he said, "an' you, big mouth . . . I don't need you. All you are is trouble."

John Lawe raised his head, tipped slightly forward, and glanced at Clyde. Almost invisibly his head moved in a commanding, upward jerk. Clyde glanced at him and then away.

Lawe's still holstered pistol lay midway to the doorway. Ten feet, perhaps. A jump and a slide. Directly under the dismally watching eye at the end of the rifle barrel. And no other choice. The big policeman's head rolled back as if in faintness. His eyes came again on Clyde, then past him, with just a flickering of changed expression, back to the killer, who was stooped, poised, watchful.

Clyde felt Kathy's arm touch him. He felt his muscles gathering, waiting some triggering impulse, and then, suddenly, shockingly, a woman screamed—just outside the screen door.

The killer swung his deadly grinning mask at the door, flicked the rifle around, and simultaneously a jingling crash came from Clyde's left, and a deep shocking roar that seemed to jar his head loose with its concussion. He heeded none of it. He went into his leaping drive, straight off the settee, driving low, letting himself fall and slide with his momentum on the slick, polished floor. His hands fell on pistol and holster, and he tore the weapon from its case, rolled on his side, thrust it straight out, and fired, not aiming, without time to aim, dimly thinking to disconcert the killer with the close muzzle blast.

In that frozen fractional instant he knew that he had missed—widely, that the killer was lifting in a strange backward leaping, clear into the kitchen end of the room, that the rifle was flung aside, that somewhere, through the curious thick deadness in his ears, a woman was screaming, endlessly, high-pitched and frantic—wordlessly screaming like an animal in pain.

The killer went back to the work counter, doubled back over that, and then slid down out of sight. He didn't have a face, anymore. Something terrible had happened to his face.

Then Clyde could hear someone shouting: "Watch it, there! Keep down out of the road!"

Clyde crouched, holding the pistol in a desperate grip. He thought of Kathy then, and looked around. She lay along the settee seat, her head in her hands, her eyes squeezed shut as if in pain.

He stared stupidly, sickeningly, rose, and turned toward her, and the screen door was flung aside, and the boyish-faced trooper, Jim Wendell, burst through, his riot gun held chest high, ready, as he took three long strides into the room. Then he stopped, and his voice was faint and faraway. "Guess that does it," he said.

Clyde opened his mouth wide and swallowed frantically, trying to get the cotton out of his ears. He touched Kathy, and she sat up, still pressing her hands to the sides of her head. "You all right?" he demanded.

She looked up at him. "Yes," she said in a dazed voice. "Yes, I'm all right, Clyde." Her arms came out to him then, and he caught her close and sat down beside her. "Oh," she said, in the voice of a frightened child. "Oh, Clyde, darling!" Then, suddenly, it was all right. He had the certainty that those arms were never going to let him go again.

A voice said: "You people all right?"

Clyde looked up. It was the young trooper. He didn't look quite so boyish. You don't kill a man with a riot gun at ten feet without showing some of it. "Damned sorry," said the trooper. "Had to shoot this thing off practically in your ears. Thought I could catch him at the door, maybe. Then the woman screamed, and all I could do was run the barrel through the window and cut loose. She's fainted," he said almost as an afterthought. "But you people are all right?"

There was some considerable confusion thereafter, which Clyde made no attempt to sort out and organize in his mind.

Sergeant John Lawe, thick-voiced and swaying a little with the pain of his smashed arm, free of the handcuffs and telling how a fisherman had found a body on the lake shore, and had caught John Lawe at the resort with the news . . . the woman who had screamed and fainted was Larry Seaforth's Aunt Margaret, who owned the next house over and was ostensibly the chaperone. Clyde knew dimly that this should mean something to him, and was faintly surprised that it did not— that Jim Wendell, Trooper Jim Wendell, had been on post, guarding the access road to the summer homes and the only one within quick range, called by John Lawe's radioed message to meet the sergeant at the nearest summer home in the first move of a house-to-house search—all this was confusion, with little light in it for Clyde Cameron. The only reality he knew was Kathy, close in his arms. "Kathy," he said. "Oh, Kathy."

Later, much later, it seemed, came the realization that he had his story—the big story.

"Come on, Kathy," he said. "We're going for a ride."

She sat close beside him on the boat thwart. It seemed they crossed the lake very quickly.

Clyde phoned in the story from the phone booth in the resort lodge lobby. He answered the excited questions almost absently. The phone booth door was open, and he held Kathy's hand through that opening. He listened, and he smiled, and felt a strong, warming surge run through him as she smiled back.

Then impatience came on him, and he said into the phone: "That's all of it. Yes, I'll give you more. But not to-night. Tomorrow, maybe. *Yes*, I said." The thought came to him then, and he said: "Here's your big story. Take this down and get it right. 'After an extended vacation at Sapphire Lake and other points, Mister and Missus Clyde Cameron will be at home to their friends, at their apartment at one-three-seven-six Vista Drive, of this city.' What do you mean, that's not news? It's the biggest news this reporter ever covered."

He hung up, then, on the protesting voice he wasn't hearing, looking at Kathy with a sudden feeling of unsureness, watchful for her reaction, asking his question in silence.

Then she smiled. "Yes, Clyde darling," she said. "It is big news. The biggest."

Almost in Clyde's ear, the phone rang. Almost he answered it, pretty certain of who it was. Then he thrust his way out of the booth. "Come on, Kathy," he said. "Let's get out of here. Let's go home."

PURSUIT

The coach passed Barron's without stopping, as the driver in the high seat up front racketed out a volley with the silk popper of his long whip. Danny McClellan rode backward, facing Merle Workman, and Danny was getting tired of looking at Merle.

Merle Workman didn't look like what he was, unless you scanned his face very closely. His eyes were a chilly light color that left you uncertain as to whether they were gray or blue, and few men cared to look directly into them long enough to satisfy themselves about it. Danny knew him very well, and he didn't like him, but there wasn't much he could do about that when he had to work with the man. *Under him, you mean,* Danny reminded himself wryly, and that made this job a particularly narrow wire to walk.

Workman wouldn't know about that, of course, because the company handled Workman with kid gloves, but Danny had his orders, very circumspect, very delicate: "Not real authority, you understand, McClellan, but well . . . you understand . . . Workman is as fine an agent as the company ever had, but he tends to be a bit impetuous. An agent is in a risky position. We understand that. A man must protect himself, but two of you should be able to bring in this man Hanseldt without any trouble. You understand?"

The coach reached the top of a knoll, and Danny looked back at the valley they'd passed, looked back at Barron's white house and a willow-fringed creek, with the Siskiyous looming beyond and Pilot Rock like a blunt thumb indicating the way to heaven.

It was a beautiful view, and much easier to look at than

Merle Workman. Danny understood, all right. Cut out the pussyfooting, and it boiled down to a mean situation. Workman was the boss—senior to Danny in years and experience. Call a spade a spade: Workman was a killer, but he was a man the express company couldn't afford to lose—and Danny was supposed to keep him from killing without offending him. *I wonder,* thought Danny, half grimly, half humorously, *if I ought to give him a little talk about flushing his birds before he fires.*

They stopped in Ashland Mills just long enough to change horses, and then bowled smoothly along the improved road that flanked Bear Creek, and still Merle Workman sat without moving, as he had all the way now, not talking, not even bothering to answer the few questions of the granger who sat beside him. Then, a few miles past Phoenix, Workman looked quickly at Danny and then back outside as the brakes squalled and the coach slowed to the sudden braking. The granger whipped off his hat and thrust his head out the window. "Rig broke down ahead," he said. Only Danny caught the subtle loosening of Merle Workman's shoulders.

The coach stopped, and Danny looked out. The rig was a light buggy, and a woman stood beside it. The hem of her full skirt was dusty, and so were her hands. The buggy sagged despondently, and a rear wheel lay in the road beside it.

The woman looked up at the driver's seat of the coach with a vexed smile and said: "The spindle nut is lost completely, Ben. I've looked all around and down the road."

"Why, now," said the coach driver, "that's too bad." The coach rocked as he started to climb down. "I've got a spare nut, but I doubt it'll fit that axle spindle."

The granger unlatched the door and got out, and, as Danny started to move, glad of the chance to escape the confinement of the coach, Workman's pale eyes silently commanded him to bide and let be, and the resentful perversity inside Danny said silently—*Go to hell!*—and he stepped out.

The driver got a heavy iron nut from the toolbox and tried it. It slipped over the threaded spindle-end without catching on the screw threads.

"Afraid I'll have to send somebody after the rig, Miss Emily," the driver said regretfully.

"Oh, fiddlesticks!" the girl said. Even in her displeasure, she had a pleasant voice, and Danny looked at her, frankly appraising.

She was fairly tall for a girl, not much more than half a head shorter than Danny himself, with blonde hair under her plain bonnet, a trim figure, and a handsome face that escaped mere prettiness. She had pushed her sleeves up to rake in the dust for the missing nut, and her expression was more considering than helpless as she looked from the coach driver to the crippled buggy.

Danny said suddenly to the driver: "You got some soft wire in that box?"

"Yes, but . . . ," the driver said, impatiently aware of his lateness.

"Get it," said Danny. He walked to the buggy and lifted up on the box bed. The granger got the wheel and slid it onto the axle and held it straight as Danny let the weight back on it. Danny slid the oversize nut over the spindle against the hub bushing, took the coil of wire from the driver's hand, and rove two layers of it about the threads, pulled an end through the cotter-pin slot, and twisted the ends. He shook the wheel, grasping it by tire and felly, and said cheerfully: "A rawhider's make-do, but it ought to hold."

The girl smiled her thanks at Danny, and the driver turned back toward the coach. But the granger said: "Looks a little shaky. Be a shame to have it leave you stranded again, Miss Emily."

Danny saw the chance and said: "I can drive her on into town. Leave the rest of that wire, just in case."

The driver turned back, instinctively scanning him with the suspicion of the local man for the stranger. He said uncomfortably, as if he would bear responsibility in case of any wrong, "I don't know. . . ."

The granger, a more open and friendly man, said: "Why not? I'd be glad to stand by myself, Miss Emily, only I'm being met at Jasonville."

The girl looked at Danny closely then, not suspicious but careful, and then she smiled her thanks. "If you're sure it will be no trouble," she said.

"None at all," said Danny, and the driver, with an air of washing his hands of it all, turned away, saying: "Load up! Late now."

Danny reached into the coach for his luggage—a worn canvas bag with a puckering cord in the neck. Workman said nothing. He wouldn't show anger or displeasure openly, Danny knew, but he also knew that the man was furious. The small, spurning gesture of Workman's foot as he nudged the duffel bag at Danny said enough. Danny gave it right back with a faint, unoffended grin and a murmured: "Thanks." And he thought, with a little relief: *Anyone will be better company than that.*

He noticed that the girl climbed to the seat unassisted while he hitched the horse back into the shafts. *No nonsense,* he said to himself. *Wonder what you'd think if you knew I'd choose your company to Workman's even if you were fat and fifty and had a wart on your nose as big as my thumb?* Then he had the grace to grin inwardly and acknowledge: *But she isn't and she hasn't, so see if you can bear up under it.*

He watched the wheel for a while, then, satisfied it would hold, said: "Didn't have a chance for introductions. My name is Danny McClellan."

She said—"I'm Emily Hanseldt."—and they bobbed their heads formally at each other, she not offering to shake hands, and then a sudden, cold, panicky shiver touched Danny's spine. He looked away and tried to ask casually: "Live in Jasonville . . . your family?"

"I do," she said. "I've just got a brother."

The cold, crawling snake looped around his ribs and made it difficult to breathe. He struggled to keep his voice on the verge of disinterest. "Know some Hanseldts in California," he lied. "Any relation?"

"No," she said consideringly, "I think not. I think we're the only ones in this part of the country."

That did it. A sour, cursing anger came up inside him, and a bitter, sardonic laughter at himself for his eagerness to escape Workman and ride with this girl. He had a sudden, overwhelming wish that he had never seen her and never would, but that was foolish. His thoughts gibed at him maliciously: *How do you make small talk in a case like this . . . tip your hat and tell her you're after her brother?*

The four miles or so to Jasonville were sheer misery. He was grateful that the girl didn't talk much. But he knew he was being almost rudely abrupt when he let her off at the Square Deal wagon shop, touched his hat, and tramped away. He thought bitterly of Workman: *Maybe the ice-water devil is right. Oh, Danny boy, that was close!*

Jasonville wasn't particularly prepossessing; he'd seen a dozen such slammed-together boom towns, and one sweeping glance took in most of it. He got a room at the Robinson Hotel, and saw Workman's scrawl a few lines above his own in the registration book. Workman had registered as Merle W. Carter, of Sacramento. Danny signed his own name and San Francisco, dumped his bag in the room, and went back to the street.

Workman was at the bar of a saloon a few doors up, talking affably enough with a man in a store suit and beaver hat, the two men looking alike as brothers, both plump and neat and obviously prosperous with the kind of prosperity that comes from other men's work. *He'd be the picture of a promoter or a saloon-keeper,* thought Danny, *if you didn't know about those two sawed-off Forty-Fours under his vest.*

Workman's chilly killer's eyes turned on Danny the moment he pushed into the room, and then they went away and back to the man he was talking to. Danny bought a drink and nursed it, not going any closer, and waited until Workman finally broke off and moved toward the door. Workman stopped in the doorway just an instant, and in a moment Danny followed.

Workman was waiting for him in the darkness of Oregon Street, and he said, with icy venom: "Don't you ever get tired of playing the fool?"

Danny held his temper and said, with forced lightness: "How old do you have to be before it turns into foolishness?"

"You're a fool at any age when you let a woman interfere with a job."

It was too good to pass up. Danny let his own inner sourness come out in a soft: "But that wasn't just any woman, Merle. That was Hanseldt's sister."

Merle Workman's neat little hand shot out and fastened on Danny's shirt front. Workman's face was up close to Danny's. "Oh, you driveling idiot!" he said.

Danny hacked with the edge of his hand and snapped Workman's hand roughly from its grip. "Don't put your hands on me, Merle," he said. "And don't call me names unless you want to follow it up."

"All right, Danny," Workman said. He did not apologize. He went on in his normal, dry, careful voice. "He isn't in town. I'll have to go after him."

Danny was alarmed by something in Workman's voice. He said carefully: "We've got no authority in this county till the sheriff honors our letter."

"Your job," Workman said promptly. Again there was the faintest thread of—what? . . . triumph, perhaps—in his almost inflectionless voice. "The sheriff isn't in town either, Danny," he added. "You see him and give him the letter, and I'll locate our man."

"All right," Danny said reluctantly. He couldn't insist without tipping Workman off about why he'd been sent along, but he had to do what he could, and he made it as casual as possible. "Be sure, Merle. Be sure he's the one we want."

Workman said quietly, as he turned away: "I don't make mistakes, Danny."

Danny said, with a little edge to his voice: "Just be damned sure, that's all, Merle."

Workman did not answer. But in a moment, a soft sound came, what might have been an amused chuckle in another man.

"You hear me?" Danny said almost harshly.

"I heard you."

The hotel dining room was full, and a dozen men waited a chance at the tables. Danny was hungry, and he went up the street, looking for an eating house, and turned in at the first one where he saw a vacant stool. He didn't see the girl until she stopped before him on the other side of the counter and said matter-of-factly: "Hello again. What will it be?"

There was a sort of nasty fascination to this whole thing, Danny thought. He knew enough to keep his nose clean. You didn't go digging around the edges of a job like this. It was better if you didn't know the kin and friends and hangers-on. Find your man, do your job, get it over. Go on to the next one and forget it. That's what you got paid for. But somehow this job wasn't shaping up like the others. "What have you got?" he asked.

"Steak, stew, or roast beef. Potatoes, beans, coffee, apple pie."

"Good. Steak, potatoes, and coffee. And a big piece of the pie."

She brought him the coffee first, without asking, then disappeared through a door at the end of the counter. It was a good steak, and he got the beans on the side, too, not dried boiled beans but fresh, tender snap beans, green and savory, with finely diced bacon. Danny ate hungrily.

Some of the diners finished, and others came in. One of them was a little drunk, and he called the girl—"Honey."—when she took his order. He looked up at her with a simper, when she served him, and he reached out to squeeze her hand as she brought the little side dish of green beans. Danny carefully laid down his knife and fork, but he picked them up again just as carefully. The drunk screamed like a woman and slapped futilely at his drenched and scalded arm, and the girl calmly set the heavy coffee pot back over its kerosene flame on the back counter. She did not even look at the man as he stared with suddenly sobered eyes at her back.

To Danny she said calmly: "More coffee?"

He looked up sharply, then grinned, and said— "Thanks."—and added hastily: "In my cup, please."

She smiled briefly and said, as she poured carefully:

"Some of them have to learn the hard way."

He thought: *So we both know that, too.* Aloud he said: "What do I owe you?"

"You did me a favor," she said. "Let's just say we're even."

He said, more brusquely than he intended: "Forget that. What do I owe you?"

"All right. Twenty cents," she said.

He laid a quarter dollar on the counter. "You forgot the pie."

She made change and pushed a nickel back to him. "It's part of the dinner."

"Then I'll buy another cup of coffee," he said. He knew he was being foolish and suddenly didn't care. He drank coffee he didn't want, and found himself the last customer in the place. He should have gone then, but he found himself asking idly: "You work here all the time?"

"It's my place. I own it."

That piqued his curiosity, and the casual question came automatically, for idle questions sometimes brought surprising answers. "You've got a brother, you said?"

"Yes."

No defensiveness, no apology—and no further explanation. Danny waited, but apparently she wasn't going to say anything more. He finished his coffee, and, as he stood to go, she came around the counter, undoing her apron strings, and followed him to the door.

He said: "I didn't mean to keep you late."

"It's just closing time," she said, as if she meant it. He went out, and she said behind him: "Good night."

He turned back and said: "Can I see you home?"

She looked at him closely. Suddenly, a yell sounded down the street. Past the hotel, someone fired a shot and whooped gleefully. She had already started to shake her head, and he tilted his head at the sound and said simply: "Just in case, is all."

She smiled then, and nodded. "Just a moment, until I get the cash drawer and my coat," she said.

He waited outside until she came. She carried a little canvas sack in one hand, and he asked: "You take your cash home with you every night?"

She gestured at the huddled street of flimsy frame buildings. "One tossed match," she said, "and half the town would go like powder."

"Hadn't thought," he said.

They walked companionably enough, not speaking. They turned at California and walked a block and a half in the darkness until she said quietly: "This is it. Thank you."

"You're welcome," he said as quietly, and stood in the dirt street until he heard her door open and close. Then he went back to the hotel.

He did not see Workman that night or the next day. He had the certain, dismal knowledge then he wouldn't see Workman until Workman came to him. The killer wolf was on the trail, and there was nothing he could do about it now.

In Danny's trade, anything done three times hard running was almost ingrained habit. Danny ate at Emily Hanseldt's place every day. In three days, there was no question about his walking her home after she closed up. In three days they were Emily and Danny, and they still walked companionably, neither confiding nor confided in, neither objecting nor requesting more than this casual relationship.

The fourth night, Danny waited until he heard her door close behind her, and then walked his usual slow stroll back to the hotel, debating whether to hunt up a game or go to bed, and decided on bed. He knew the moment he touched the knob to his door that Workman was in the room.

Danny wasn't sure how he knew. That was something that had come with his trade over time. He knew the moment he touched the knob, and he said softly—"Coming in, Merle."—so that Workman could hear his voice, and then he went on into the dark room and closed the door.

Workman said—"Danny."—without question or surprise, and lighted a match and touched it to the lamp wick. He put the chimney back in its brackets, standing with his back to Danny, and Danny thought desperately: *He's done it . . . he's caught him and killed him.* And then Workman turned without looking directly at him and said: "He's a roamer. Rock Point, Grave Creek, Steamboat Creek, Applegate. He moves around."

Workman turned back to fiddle with the lamp, and Danny thought savagely: *Damn you, quit playing with me!*

Then Workman said in his dry, matter-of-fact voice: "You've seen the sheriff?"

Danny said slowly, carefully watching Workman's face: "Yes. He honored the letter." He took the folded paper from his pocket and shook out the two deputy's badges.

"Good," Workman said heartily. "Good. Now we get down to business." He put out a hand, and Danny gave him one of the badges, and Workman grinned his thin, malicious grin and flipped the emblem in the air like a coin. "Let's go," he said.

Danny looked down at the badge in his own hand, and, for perhaps the fiftieth time in four days, he asked himself how he'd got started at this business. And for the fiftieth time, he had no sure answer. Maybe it was the streak of wildness he'd had from the first day he walked, a way he had of waking to each day with a little tingle of excitement as if this were the day something really big was going to happen. It hadn't happened at home, and he had simply left one day when he was fifteen years old. It hadn't happened when he rode after another man's cattle for money, either, and he'd drifted in and out of a lot of strange places since. He was quick and tough and almost nerveless by the time he's served his apprenticeships in other trades, and this was the first time he'd really felt reluctance.

Without his really thinking about them, the words came out: "Merle, don't take this one all the way."

Workman said, without emphasis or malice: "Just because you've been squiring his sister every night since I left . . . I told you not to be a fool, Danny."

Danny said bitterly: "Forget that. All I ask is. . . ."

"He'll have his chance," Workman said tonelessly.

"That I know," said Danny. "You'll make his chance. You'll blind him with that smooth face of yours, and you'll turn your back on him, and he'll make a break, and then you'll kill him."

"I never drew first on a man in my life," Workman said. His eyes, as colorless as two chips of ice, were blank and unrevealing. "Don't say something you'll regret, Danny."

There was no mercy in the man, Danny knew, and he knew now that Workman had his mind made up.

Danny sighed, a slow, regretful, resigned sound. He dropped the badge in his pocket. He drew his gun and clicked the cylinder around, inspecting the bright brass caps on the nipples. Then he cocked the gun and leveled it, and said in a perfectly flat, emotionless voice: "Put your hands behind your head, Merle." He made his voice quiet, but inside him a vaulting excitement began to rise.

Merle Workman did not curse or cry out. A faint match flame of light began to show behind the polished chips of ice in his eye sockets. He raised his hands, slowly, and locked his fingers behind his head.

Danny said softly: "I'm taking your pistols, Merle." He almost pulled the trigger then, for that was the moment. The light blazed in Workman's pale eyes, and the faint movement of automatic protest started. Then the light dulled, and Danny reached out with his left hand and flipped up the points of Workman's vest and got the two .44s with rammer and linkage removed completely and the barrels cut down to three inches. He did not touch him otherwise, or let his own pistol come within arm's length of Workman's body.

"All right, Merle," he said. "Now we'll go."

Workman said, almost pleadingly: "Danny. . . ."

"Let's go," Danny said, and they went down to get the horses Workman had ready.

As they rode into the darkness, Merle said quietly: "I don't have to show you where he is, Danny."

"You'll show me," said Danny. They rode through the ghostly mystery of the timbered cañons, south, and a little east. The two .44s gouged at Danny's belly where he'd thrust them out of the way under his belt, and he began to wish he'd left them behind. The moon came up, high and cold and not quite fully round, and Merle Workman said: "He's killed a man, Danny He shot Jimmy Davis out of the seat when he got the express box. Jimmy was a friend of mine."

"You never had a friend in your life," Danny said flatly.

They came to a stream, and the horses drank. "How much farther?" Danny asked.

"Over the next ridge," Workman said tonelessly. "Now give me my pistols, Danny. You've carried this foolishness far enough."

"We'll do this one my way," Danny said. "I got no orders to kill him."

Workman said disgustedly: "Damn it, don't preach me a sermon, Danny!"

"I'm not preaching," Danny said. "I'm telling you. I know how you've made your reputation, Merle. Why do you suppose the express company sent me along with you on this one? You've brought in too many dead ones."

Workman said, almost mildly: "I don't believe that. Besides, I couldn't very well argue with a man who drew a gun on me, could I?"

Danny cried: "Damn it, Merle, I know you, and I'm sick of you! I'm not saying you're always wrong in this. Some of them you've killed deserved it. But I can't stomach any more of that pose, Merle. You walk the earth like a fallen god, and men step back from those guns under your vest. Take them away from you, Merle, and you're nothing . . . you're less than nothing."

Workman said, in a voice that was incredibly tired: "I'll kill you, Danny."

"No you won't," Danny said. "Because I know you, now. You never grew up, Merle. You were a kid with an itch that came up with the sun, and you've chased something all your life. You've never caught it, and you never will, and you've tried to cover it with something else. You've hunted men like rabbits . . . and my God, you didn't even have the guts to do that out in the open. You've hidden behind a job as agent for the company, and you've made the reputation of a manhunting wolf . . . but you and I know how it was done. You pushed and you hounded them, and when you closed in, you came at them with your hands empty and looked away. And when they bit on your bait, you killed them."

He looked at Workman, the dull, white, lower half of his face showing, the eyes hidden under the black splash of shadow from the moonlight. "What does it do for you, Merle, to kill a man? To see him go down kicking under your guns? Soothe the itch, does it, Merle?"

Merle Workman cried in a sobbing voice—"Damn you, Danny!"—and lashed at him with his fist, crowding his horse in on Danny's. Danny fended off the blow with an upflung arm, and then Workman's clawing hand caught at his collar, and, as the horse shied away, his weight came on Danny, and they fell together.

Danny rolled and shook off Workman's weight, and said: "I can whip you, Merle. Don't be a fool."

But Workman came in again, clawing insanely, and Danny hit him lightly, not really wanting to hurt him, and then he felt the hands at his belly, and knew he'd done it all wrong. Workman had fooled him again. Workman hadn't broken. For Workman had one of the .44s now, and he could light a match at ten feet with them with either hand. Even as he fell back before the light blow, Workman's eyes were on Danny, cold and malicious with sardonic laughter, and the snub-nosed .44 was coming around with Workman's thumb on the hammer.

Danny said—"Don't!"—even as he drew in an unthinking motion, thrusting out his own gun and thumbing off the shot as the .44 roared from an arm's length away, and then Workman wheeled half away from him and made a crying sound and shot the .44 into the ground again and fell forward almost into the creek.

Merle Workman looked as old as sin. His grayish whiskers had sprouted since last morning's shave, and he looked old and tired and sick. His polished ice-chip eyes, with that little match-light of fire behind them, came on Danny, and Workman said very softly: "Oh, you lucky damned fool, Danny!" Then he died.

Danny turned and walked blindly into his own horse, caught at the saddle horn, and clung there for a moment, feeling a vague sickness inside and a dull wonder whether his legs were going to hold him up. For a moment, the temptation to forget the rest of this job was almost overwhelming. It would be so easy to do it that way, take Workman back in and resign—turn it over to another company agent. Nobody could blame him.

Then he thought of Workman, and what he had become, lying to himself with little half lies, cutting corners with his conscience, and he swung up into the saddle and lifted the reins.

Emily, he thought, *I've got to do it. I've got to do this one before I quit. Maybe you won't be able to see it. But I've got to do it. If I don't, someday I'll look at you and tell myself I bought you, that night, with what I didn't do. So I've got to do it, Emily. I'll have to take in your brother, and then I'll have to make it up with you. We'll have time after today—a lifetime.*

He crossed the ridge, and in the faint early light he saw the cabin, a rough, shake-roofed shack, sleeping in the new day. He rode up slowly, until he was close enough, then drew the gun and held it across his thigh. He took a deep breath and called: "John Hanseldt, come out!"

Then he swung down, the gun a plainly visible warning in his fist, and waited.